# GET A

# EE

**WITH JUST**

**E:**

◆ **Hotel Discounts** up to 60% at home and abroad ◆ **Travel Service -** Guaranteed lowest published airfares plus 5% cash back on tickets ◆ **$25 Travel Voucher** ◆ **Sensuous Petite Parfumerie** collection ◆ **Insider Tips Letter** with sneak previews of upcoming books

***You'll get a FREE personal card, too.***
***It's your passport to all these benefits–and to even more great gifts & benefits to come!***

*There's no club to join. No purchase commitment. No obligation.*

SR-PP6A

***"Are you suggesting that we live together?" Katherine gasped.***

"Why not?" Alex asked.

"A single man and woman living together are no match for a married couple who live on a ranch, have sufficient income and have two other children, which proves they know what they're doing as parents."

"All right, Miss-High-And-Mighty, then what you're suggesting is that we should get married?"

Katherine gasped.

He'd only said it to get her dander up, but getting married wasn't such a bad idea. "I'm not the one who made the suggestion."

For a second Katherine only stared at him. He was actually considering this!

"Are you nuts?" she asked, though suddenly she was noting things like his crystal eyes, his perfect chin, his sculptured body.... Good Lord! Now she was considering it!

Dear Reader,

Favorite author Kasey Michaels starts off the month with another irresistible FABULOUS FATHER in *The Dad Next Door*. Quinn Patrick was enjoying a carefree bachelor life-style until Maddie Pemberton and her son, Dillon, moved next door. And suddenly Quinn was faced with the prospect of a ready-made family!

A BUNDLE OF JOY helps two people find love in *Temporarily Hers* by Susan Meier. Katherine Whitman would do anything to win custody of her nephew, Jason, even marry playboy Alex Cane—temporarily. But soon Katherine found herself wishing their marriage was more than a temporary arrangement....

Favorite author Anne Peters gives us the second installment in her miniseries FIRST COMES MARRIAGE. Joy Cooper needed a *Stand-in Husband* to save her reputation. Who better for the job than Paul Mallik, the stranger she had rescued from the sea? Of course, love was never supposed to enter the picture!

The spirit of the West lives on in Pat Montana's *Storybook Cowboy*. Jo McPherson didn't want to trust Trey Covington, the upstart cowboy who stirred her heart. If she wasn't careful, she might find herself in love with the handsome scoundrel!

This month, we're delighted to present our PREMIERE AUTHOR, Linda Lewis, debuting with a fun-filled, fast-paced love story, *Honeymoon Suite*. And rounding out the month, look for Dani Criss's exciting romance, *Family Ties*.

Happy Reading!

Anne Canadeo, Senior Editor

Please address questions and book requests to:
Silhouette Reader Service
U.S.: 3010 Walden Ave., P.O. Box 1325, Buffalo, NY 14269
Canadian: P.O. Box 609, Fort Erie, Ont. L2A 5X3

# TEMPORARILY HERS

Susan Meier

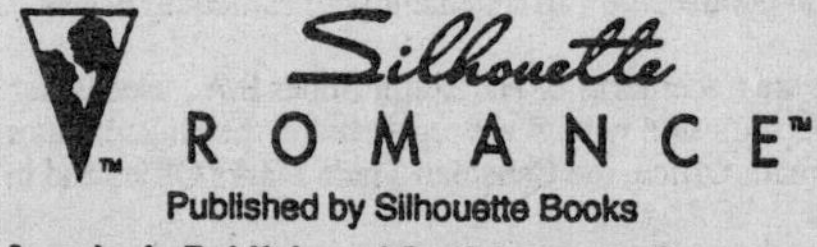


Published by Silhouette Books
America's Publisher of Contemporary Romance

SILHOUETTE BOOKS

ISBN 0-373-19109-X

TEMPORARILY HERS



This edition published by arrangement with Harlequin Books S.A.



**Printed in U.S.A.**

**Books by Susan Meier**

Silhouette Romance

*Stand-in Mom* #1022
*Temporarily Hers* #1109

Silhouette Desire

*Take the Risk* #567

---

## *SUSAN MEIER*

is a wife, mother and romance writer. She firmly believes that, in romance, sometimes it's not what you say but how you say it. Therefore, the most simple events can be made to sound beautiful.

When she's not writing or working, she's probably watching movies, which she counts as one of her greatest interests, or reading.

Dear Reader,

Because I'd always wanted a career, I never thought about becoming a mother. In fact, I didn't pay attention to other people's babies or children and found myself totally unprepared—but in a good way. The whole experience for me has been like a wonderful adventure.

When my son Michael was born, I was amazed by how tiny his toes were. His skin felt so much like velvet that I spent hours touching it, experiencing absolute wonder that this little ball of softness was actually a person. My daughter, Sarah, brought us the joy of buying ruffled-rump tights, frilly dresses and baby dolls, not to mention naming all our blankets. And after reading the "little chick" book every night for a year, I finally figured out that my son Allen (Spunky) loved it because the big red chicken reminded him of me.

Having children brought the magic and wonder back into my life. Not just because they help me to look at things as if for the first time, but also because they got me to do things I didn't think I wanted to do—like ride water slides and roller coasters.

My children are teenagers now and the challenges are different. They raid my wallet and try my patience, but they're still wonderful. Fun. I know my life wouldn't have been half as exciting without them.

Sincerely,

Susan Meier

# *Chapter One*

"Unfortunately, that isn't the end of the docket for this case."

Confused by Judge Arnold Black's last statement, Katherine Whitman and Alex Cane, opponents in a custody battle for their nephew, Jason, snuck a peek at each other.

Looking at Alex Cane's well-cut silk suit and his shiny Italian loafers, Katherine speculated that Jason's rich, powerful uncle had allowed his battery of lawyers to file yet another round of documents to jam the case with so much paper, the judge would rule in his favor just to get rid of him.

Glancing at the uncomplicated lines of Katherine's navy blue linen dress and her sleek, shoulder-length auburn hair, Alex decided Jason's prim-and-proper aunt must have felt the need to sling a little more mud. She'd probably filed another piece of legal garbage based on the same kind of tabloid dirt she'd used against him in her own petition for custody.

Judge Black cleared his throat. "It seems, Mr. Cane, that your sister, Marissa Peligrini, has also filed for custody of your nephew, Jason."

Alex felt his eyes widen with surprise and he gasped, "What?" before he could stop to consider the ramifications.

Katherine immediately glanced at him. His straight sandy brown hair fell to his forehead. His green eyes narrowed and grew bright with fury even as his mouth, a generous mouth with plump lips, firmed into a thin line. Obviously, he wasn't expecting this any more than she was. Quickly—to prevent the impending angry outburst from Alex Cane—Katherine faced the judge and said, "But I thought Jason didn't have any relatives other than Alex and me."

"Not according to documentation that accompanied Mrs. Peligrini's petition. She sent birth certificates and other pertinent papers that prove that she and Jason's father were brother and sister."

"Marissa may have been Ryan's sister, Your Honor," Alex's lawyer, a slick Philadelphia type, argued casually, "but we can prove that because of an underlying animosity, Mrs. Peligrini and Ryan Cane did not have a close relationship. Because of that, Mrs. Peligrini has never even met Jason."

Awestruck, Katherine sat back on her chair. Alex Cane might not have been expecting this, but his lawyer was and had a defense all ready. The sister was legitimate. That much was clear. Katherine wasn't surprised or upset that her free-spirited brother-in-law hadn't told his wife's family that he had a sister. Ryan was like that. The less he spoke, the less he had to lie. It was Alex Cane's reaction to that sister that had Katherine's nerves jumping.

"Mrs. Peligrini mentions in her petition that she's never met Jason," the judge agreed. "But Marissa and Tom Peligrini bring other items to the table. Marissa and Tom have been married for almost fifteen years. They have a son and a daughter, both of whom are only slightly older than Jason. The Peligrinis live on a ranch in Montana, and not only is Mr. Peligrini gainfully employed, the income from the ranch appears to be significant."

Katherine felt her heart stop. "You're going to give Jason to these people, aren't you?" she said, completely shocked by the unexpected turn of events. She'd entered the hearing this morning fully anticipating a short, simple proceeding after which the judge would immediately award her custody. Sexy, arrogant Alex Cane might have money and power. He might be a smart man who created a television dynasty in spite of his tremendously humble roots. And he might even be a hell of a lot bolder than Katherine, but Katherine was a normal, sensible person, more capable of raising a child.

That is, until the introduction of *Mr. and Mrs.* Tom Peligrini.

"Yes, when I rule, custody may be awarded to the Peligrinis. They have a lot to offer Jason," the judge said, confirming Katherine's worst fear. "However, I'm not actually going to set the hearing or write the custody order until the first of August, with the stipulation that Jason must meet with the Peligrinis at least once before the actual hearing."

Numb, Katherine said nothing, but Alex Cane leaned across the desk. He combed the shiny strands of hair off his forehead, accenting his brilliant, grass-green eyes that were still shooting fire. "Let me see if I have this straight.

You're going to give custody of *my* nephew to a sister who didn't even associate with Ryan, and your only justification is that she's married?"

"No. My justification is that she's stable."

"I'm stable," Alex protested indignantly.

"You're rich," the judge countered dryly. "You're about as far from stable as I've seen in this court without being in a position to pass sentence."

"Then at the very least she's stable," Alex argued, thrusting his thumb in Katherine's direction.

"She's broke," the judge said quietly, turning to face Katherine. "You helped your sister with doctor bills, didn't you?"

"And now I'm being punished for it?"

"No," the judge said, then sighed. "I'm sorry it sounds that way. The truth of the matter is, my purpose in warning you of my feelings about this case is to let you know what you're up against. And, hopefully, give either one or both of you the opportunity to show me you could provide Jason with just as stable a home as Marissa Peligrini can."

"You mean, if we come in here in August and we tell you I'm giving Ms. Whitman money," Alex proposed, "then you'd rule in her favor?"

The judge shook his head. "Money is only part of the issue. Ms. Whitman travels—three days a week. Money would help her provide overnight child care for Jason, but it wouldn't give him the kind of stable home life a two-year-old needs." He paused, shook his head. "Jason needs security more than anything else. Particularly in light of the fact that both of his parents died within the last six months."

"And don't bother arguing that you'll change jobs, Ms. Whitman," he continued. "Not only is our local economy down so far you'd have desperate trouble finding another position, but the last thing Jason needs right now is to live with someone who's adjusting to a new work environment."

The room became as still as dawn in a forest. The judge glanced at his watch. "I have another hearing scheduled in fifteen minutes, and I need this time in my office to prepare for the next case, so if you have no more questions of me, I have to go. However, I know this is something of a shock for you, so you may continue to use this hearing room, if you wish."

He rose and left the silent office. When the door closed with a soft click, Alex's lawyer snapped his briefcase locks, then rose. "We'll change his mind at the hearing."

As if not wanting to be outdone, Munro Goldstein, Katherine's rather stiff young lawyer, turned to her. "We'll present our case at the hearing."

Alex grabbed his lawyer's wrist. "Didn't you hear a word the judge said?"

"Yes. He said that based on the petitions he's received, he thinks he's awarding custody of your nephew to a sister you hardly know and whom Jason doesn't know at all. So we'll change his mind at the hearing."

"And what if we don't, Ralph?" Alex asked.

Ralph Fasulo looked completely perplexed by the possibility that he might lose the case, but when he saw Alex was deadly serious, he shrugged. "Then we'll appeal."

"But by the time our appeal comes to trial," Alex said logically, "won't the judge's order have already sent Jason to live with Marissa?"

"Maybe."

"So, even if we appeal, won't our chances of winning be slim to none, since no judge would want to yank Jason away from a new home with two parents?"

"Maybe," Munro said, butting in when Alex's attorney would have made the same conclusion. "But if we file a strong enough appeal, we can get an injunction to preclude Jason's leaving at all...."

"If we can't win the original case, how can we file a strong enough appeal to get an injunction?" Katherine asked. "Just like Judge Black said, the thing Jason needs in his life right now is security. Even if the case would be assigned to a different judge, any judge is going to be trying to provide him with security...."

"That's a chance we'll have to take, Ms. Whitman," Alex's lawyer said.

"Not with *my* nephew," Alex said angrily.

"Or mine," Katherine said, standing up as she spoke. She took a few steps and stood behind Alex Cane's chair, uncomfortably realizing that somehow or another she and Alex Cane had gone from being enemies to being allies. They'd never met, never even spoken, yet here they were... allies.

Alex turned and glanced at Katherine. An odd, awkward feeling settled in the air, and for some reason he thought of a schoolmarm siding with the town gambler. The analogy made him smile. She did look like a schoolmarm. Prim. Proper. Ridiculously right about everything. Probably the only person in the world that Marissa couldn't criticize or even find fault with....

Maybe it wouldn't be such a bad idea for them to join forces.

Alex spun to face his counsel. "I think we have to figure out a better way to handle this than hoping we'll change Judge Black's mind at the hearing and hoping we'll win an appeal if we don't change his mind."

"Okay, we will," Alex's lawyer agreed. "Let's brainstorm back at my office."

Alex shook his head. "No. I think Ms. Whitman and I should stay right here and discuss this."

"Fine," Ralph said, tossing his briefcase back to the judge's desk as he fell into a seat again.

"Without you," Alex said pointedly.

This stopped him cold. For a minute, he didn't say anything, but once the full import of Alex's statement sunk in, he said, "But, Alex—"

"There are some things that need to be handled personally, privately," Alex interrupted before his lawyer could say any more. "Katherine and I are Jason's closest living relatives, and no matter what the judge thinks *he* wants to decide, Katherine and I still have decisions to make. At best, we deserve the opportunity to come up with our options and a strategy to put those options into action. At worst, we deserve the opportunity to commiserate. And I think it would all go a little better, a little more honestly, if we had this discussion alone. Right, Katherine?"

He turned to her then, looking up at her over his shoulder, and Katherine felt her heart flip-flop. His formerly scowling face was now smiling. His full, lush lips had winged into a boyish grin that should have looked out of place settled among the classic features of his strong-boned face, but instead actually put the finishing touch on his style—a style millions had tried to copy without success. From the top of his head to the tips of his black loafers, Alex Cane was the epitome of perfection. Even in a spectacular suit, he looked cool, comfortable. His sandy brown hair was soft and shiny. His clear green eyes sparkled. His skin held a healthy glow that was part suntan, part effervescence. Alex Cane was, quite simply, absolutely gorgeous.

And rich.

And powerful.

If you didn't get that from the clothes he wore, or the confidence he exuded, all one had to do was look at his smile. He smiled beautifully. Perfectly. So perfectly, in fact, that Katherine knew she was staring.

She swallowed hard. She wasn't really staring because he was handsome... gorgeous. She was staring because the situation was very confusing. Right? The last thing she expected from this morning was to emerge from this hearing on the same side as the man her sister absolutely hated. And now they weren't just calling out sides, declaring loyalties, he was asking her to help him form a plan.

She drew a long breath. Neither one of them could afford to lose this hearing to a woman who lived on the other side of the country, but it wouldn't be too smart to jump into an alliance without the advice of counsel. She turned to Munro. "I don't think it would hurt for me to take a minute and talk with Mr. Cane, do you?"

Munro shrugged. "Quite frankly, Katherine, it almost appears as if the turn of events has put you on the same side." As he said those words, he caught her wrist and pulled her a few feet away from Alex Cane's chair. "Even more frankly," he whispered, "you stand a much better chance of getting shared custody with a man who can help you with child support than you do of getting custody alone." He paused, pursed his lips then pulled her a little farther away from Alex, his voice dropping even lower in volume. "This may actually be the best thing that could have happened to you. So, don't blow it by losing your temper because Jessica didn't like him."

She drew a long, patient breath. "I won't."

Munro set his hand on top of her hand. "Promise me, or I'm staying."

"You really think I need him that badly?"

Munro sighed. "Actually, I don't think you stand a snowball's chance in hell without him."

"Why didn't you tell me this before?" Katherine whispered.

"Because your sister just died," Munro pointed out logically. "You have no money, and a rich, successful, incredibly powerful relative from Jason's father's side was taking you to court. I thought you had enough trouble without hearing my interpretation of how the case would eventually pan out."

"But I was paying you to hear how the case would eventually pan out!"

"I wasn't going to send you a bill," Munro said calmly, then turned away from her. "Well, Ralph," he said to Alex Cane's attorney. "I could use a cup of coffee. How about you?"

"Might as well," Ralph Fasulo said as he rose from his seat beside Alex Cane. He began to stroll away, but reconsidered and faced Alex again. "No selling the ranch, all right?"

"I don't own a ranch," Alex said, smiling, his bright, lively eyes twinkling with merriment. "I'd like to own a ranch, but you and my investment counselors seem to think they're a bad risk right now."

"They are," Ralph agreed, then turned away again. "Just don't make any deals that I can't in good conscience take to a judge."

"But, Ralph, you're so good at making judges see the merit in my ideas."

Ralph Fasulo released a sound that was a cross between a snort and a laugh. He led Munro Goldstein out of the judge's chambers, Munro closed the door and Katherine found herself standing not more than two feet away from the richest, most powerful man in broadcasting.

"You know, there are basically three kinds of negotiating styles," Alex said, as he toyed with a paper clip he'd found on the hearing room desk. "You can outthink your opponent, you can charm him," he said, and finally glanced up at her. "Or you can just plain whip the hell out of him."

"And you had every intention of whipping the hell out of me, didn't you?" Katherine said boldly, her face the picture of controlled fury, as she began to see why Jessica absolutely hated this man. He was so arrogant, he still didn't understand that he wasn't in any better position than she was.

"This wasn't much of a contest."

"Well, you sanctimonious fool," Katherine said, though some of what Munro had just said to her was sinking in, and she was starting to feel like David coming up against Goliath. "If you were any better of a guardian than I am, you wouldn't have to worry about your sister, Marissa, right now. But the truth of the matter is, you may have money, but your life-style stinks. How in the world did you think you were going to raise a child when you can't even keep your escapades out of the papers?"

"I keep myself *in* the papers," he stated casually, smiling a little bit at his own craftiness, "because it keeps people interested in me and curious about the programs I produce. It's simple PR...small potatoes compared to the fact that you can't even afford to put food on the table."

"I can afford to put food on the table."

"Oh, yeah, at the risk of the roof you'd put over Jason's head," he countered, then sighed. "Look, this isn't getting us anywhere. And you're not the enemy anymore."

"I may not be your enemy, Mr. Cane," Katherine reminded him, "but I'm not quite so sure your status has changed."

"All right," Alex said quietly, masterfully. "Then let's just get to the bottom line. The only hope you had of winning custody of Jason was on the basis that my life-style might be a little... unusual."

"Unusual?" Katherine said in a gasp. "Your name's been linked with half the women in the country."

"Jealous?" he said, but he smiled. The dimples in his cheeks shifted the lines and planes of his face in such a way that he looked so damned handsome, Katherine instantly understood why his name had been linked with half the women in the United States. She also realized the man was so conceited, his picture should be in the dictionary under "vain."

"Exasperated is a better word for it," Katherine said calmly, though she had the sudden urge to shake some sense into him. "You have enough money that it really shouldn't matter to you if Jason is moved across the country to Montana. Not only could you easily afford the airfare, but I bet you own a plane or two and could visit anytime you wanted. But I don't. And I'm the only person, aside from daycare aides and his playmates at daycare, that Jason's seen with any kind of regularity since he was born. I'm the only person he really knows. He doesn't even think of my parents as family because he hasn't seen them much since they live in California. And now the court is going to take him away from me... *away from me* because I don't have enough money to support him."

Alex shifted on his chair. Now that he'd confirmed that she really understood how limited her options were, he had planned to suggest shared custody, but from the agitated way she was pacing, he wasn't quite sure she wouldn't turn on him for mentioning it. All things considered, his only recourse might be to make shared custody look like it was her idea.

He cleared his throat. "You know, it's funny. If you had my money or if I had your reputation for being honest and trustworthy, neither one of us would be in this predicament right now."

"Yeah, but I don't have your money and you don't have my reputation. And, let's face it, neither one of them's transferrable."

He thought for a second and decided she hadn't gotten the big picture yet. He dropped one more bread crumb, hoping to lead her to the right trail. "Realistically, I could give you money."

"The judge didn't think so. He thinks money's only part of my problem. He may not be questioning my reputation, but he doesn't see me as stable because I'm never home. My job requires that I travel."

"That's right. The judge did mention that." Alex sighed, then shook his head. "I keep forgetting that normal people still have to go out into the world, because I don't go to work anymore. I work from my house. I set it up so that I can run my entire conglomerate from my library. I got damned sick and tired of traveling...."

His own vision of shared custody took on a clearer, better dimension and he forgot all about making this her idea. "Wait a minute, wait a minute. If you, Jason and I lived in the same house, not only could you act as the stabilizing influence in Jason's life, but I'd be home when you weren't home...."

Katherine's mouth dropped open slightly. "Are you suggesting that we live together?"

"Why not? If we lived together, I'd pay all the expenses, and it wouldn't matter how much money you made, where you spent it or even if you traveled. Because those are all the things I'd take care of."

"And I'd take care of what?" Katherine asked skeptically, as she marched over to stand in front of him. She slammed her hands on her hips and the crimson nails of her slender fingers made a stark, sexy fan across the skirt of her linen dress. One side of her hair had been pushed behind her ear and the way the free side angled forward made her look daring and dangerous. Her crimson lips bowed downward in a stern frown, but her cocoa eyes were bright, challenging, exciting.

Alex could think of about thirteen things she could handle easily for him, but he knew that if he alluded to even the most innocent she would undoubtedly slap his face. He licked his suddenly dry lips. Though he hadn't picked up on it in the first twenty minutes they'd spent in this hearing room, Alex suddenly saw she was one dazzling woman.

Despite the potential slap in the face, he would chance asking, or maybe suggesting, a completely different course for this bargain...that is, if it weren't for Jason.

Jason's welfare was just a tad too important and too serious to be risking it for a woman. He cleared his throat again. "Well, it goes without saying that I have this off-color reputation that the judge doesn't seem to like."

"That's putting it mildly."

"And your presence would be the stabilizing influence that the judge seems to want."

Though she appeared to understand his logic, Katherine shook her head. "A single man and woman living together are no match for a married couple who live on a ranch, have sufficient income and also have two other children, which proves they know what they're doing as parents."

Now Alex knew why it took so long to realize she was sexy. She might be attractive, but she had the tone and demeanor of a wet blanket—a prudish wet blanket—a prudish, old-maid wet blanket. "Has anyone ever told you you're a pessimist?"

"Many people, but I like to consider myself a realist."

"Most pessimists do. All right, Miss-High-And-Mighty, what do you suggest? We should get married?"

Katherine gasped. "Are you nuts?"

He'd only said that to get her dander up, but when he thought about it, getting married wasn't such a bad idea. It wasn't exactly in his plan of things to do for the year, but it would help them get Jason, and at this moment that's all he cared about. "I'm not the one who made the suggestion."

For a second Katherine only stared at him. He wasn't nervous or quaking. He wasn't confused. He wasn't looking at her as if she were crazy. Good God! Was he actually considering this!

"Are you nuts?" she said again, though suddenly she was noting things like his crystal eyes, his perfect chin, his sculptured body... Good Lord! Now *she* was considering it!

He smiled knowingly. "It's really not such a horrible suggestion, is it?"

She turned away in a huff. "Mr. Cane, I have absolutely no intention of marrying you."

"Why not?" he asked, but his voice came from a spot about an inch and a half above her ear. Warm sensations rippled through her. She jumped away from him.

"Because when I get married, I'm getting married for real."

"And you don't care that we're about to lose Jason? In other words, getting married for real is more important to you than keeping Jason with the family that he knows."

"There are other ways around this."

"Like living together?"

"I don't think the judge will go for that, but he may go for shared custody."

Alex shook his head. "You didn't hear a damned word he said, did you?"

"I heard every word he said."

"You didn't hear the implications, then. This judge is looking to provide Jason with security and stability. Judge Black is old, and he's old-fashioned. I personally don't believe he's going to find shared custody better than my sister Marissa's happy home."

Katherine blew her breath out in a long sigh. "Probably not."

"I also don't think he's going to see two single people sharing a house to share a child as an acceptable alternative."

This time she shook her head. "No, I think you're right again."

"Our only hope is to get married."

Katherine spent another thirty seconds just looking at the man across the room from her. As a negotiator for a solid waste company, a marketing representative who not only found the clients, she negotiated their contracts, Katherine knew very well how to interpret the intentions of the people with whom she spoke. Right now she could quite clearly see that Alex Cane was one-hundred-percent, dry-bone serious.

"I can't believe it means so little to you to give up your right to an honest marriage."

"I can't believe your right to an honest marriage means more to you than raising Jason."

Frustrated, Katherine dropped her head to her hands and let her fingers comb through the thick straight strands of her blunt-cut hair. "You're confusing me."

"No, I don't think there's anything to be confused about. I think we have one choice and one choice only."

"You won't run shared custody by the judge?" Katherine offered seriously.

"If he rejects it, we won't get the chance to try getting married. The judge will know our marriage is a sham, and he'll reject that, too."

Incredulous, Katherine only stared at him again. "Are you saying we're not just supposed to get married, but we're supposed to pretend we're in love?"

Calmly, casually, Alex said, "It won't work any other way. The judge has got to think that trying to resolve this between ourselves put us in such a position that we fell in love or he won't consider us any better than if we were merely living together to share custody."

"But that's all we'd be doing...."

"I know that and you know that," Alex pointed out emphatically. "But the judge *can't* know that."

Suddenly, clearly, Katherine not only understood what he was saying, but he made sense, and in an odd, unorthodox sort of way she agreed. The only way they would get custody of Jason would be to provide a better, more stable home than Marissa, and the only way they could do that was as a married couple.

She swallowed. "I'll think about it."

Alex smiled. Katherine's toes curled. "The way I see this, Ms. Whitman, we don't have much of a choice. *You* don't have much of a choice."

Once again, Katherine only stared at him. Then she shook her head in wonder. "I always have a choice, Mr. Cane. Always have options." She turned away. "I just haven't thought of them yet."

## *Chapter Two*

When Katherine reached the day-care center that afternoon, Jason didn't wait for her car to roll to a stop before he began scrambling down the porch steps to greet her. As always, her heart burst with joy at his eagerness when she came to pick him up. He had become so dear to her with his big green eyes and shaggy brown hair, that Katherine couldn't remember what her life was like before he came into it. Today, however, Katherine felt an excruciating stab of pain when she saw him running to meet her, because she realized that unless she thought of a way to convince the judge to let her keep Jason, she was going to lose him. Maybe forever.

But even worse, she would be the next on a long list of people who'd already let Jason down. He was two. He didn't understand his mother's fatal illness any more than he understood his father's accident six months ago. All he knew was that his parents weren't around anymore. That they'd abandoned him. And if the judge sent Jason to

Montana, he would think that Katherine had abandoned him as well.

Katherine opened her car door and slid out. "Hi, bud," she said, ruffling sandy brown hair that was poker straight and every bit as shiny as his uncle Alex's, before she looked down into his bright green eyes. "How'd it go today?"

He blinked at her but didn't say anything. Katherine picked him up and hugged him, hoping to transmit to him that somehow, some way, everything was going to be all right, even though she really wasn't sure that it would be. "Okay, go say goodbye to everybody, while I talk to Mrs. Kalinyak."

As always, Mrs. Kalinyak reported that Jason was quiet and well behaved, though he still didn't join in any of the games and activities unless specifically told he must do so. Worse, while the other children napped, Jason did nothing but stare out the window.

Jason wasn't old enough to be a particularly talkative child, but it troubled Katherine when he went through these days when he said absolutely nothing at all. The psychologist she'd consulted had told her not to worry about it, and to give Jason the time he needed to deal with his mother's absence in his life, but it broke Katherine's heart to see him suffer this way. There was a part of her that wondered if he really did need a home like the kind Alex's sister, Marissa, could provide, and another part of her that knew he would absolutely die if the judge took him away from Katherine and forced him to move two thousand miles away from the only home he'd ever known. He may not be talking to her, but he was glad to see her every afternoon at six, and Katherine knew in her soul that this child needed her.

* * *

When the last of their dinner was gone, the painful, grief-stricken silence still stretched between them. "I'll tell you what, bud," Katherine said, smiling sweetly at her nephew. "Why don't you go watch cartoons while Aunt Katherine washes the dishes alone tonight?"

Once again, he refrained from talking. Katherine helped him out of his booster seat and, head bowed, he slowly walked into the living room. Katherine bit back a sigh. She hated to see him like this and knew in her heart that unless she came up with something really big, the judge was going to send him away.

After gathering the dinner utensils from the table, Katherine began stacking them in the dishwasher. The doorbell rang, and she grabbed a cloth to dry her hands. But before she finished, an ear-piercing squeal exploded from her living room and hit her with the same force as an icy knife in her chest would. Not taking time to recognize it was a squeal of delight, not fear, Katherine bolted into her living room.

She stepped over the threshold just in time to see Jason gasp with pleasure. "Uncle Alex!" he cried, flinging himself in the arms of the man who was stooped on her doorstep.

"Hey, kid," Alex said, as he caught his nephew. The flowers he held in his right hand drifted to the floor, forgotten as Jason hugged the notorious Alex Cane and poured out a stream of chatter so long, one would have thought he'd been waiting for Alex to arrive at his door.

Watching their emotional and joyous reunion, Katherine didn't know whether to sigh with relief that finally someone could make Jason smile again . . . or scream. Because the last person she wanted around, clouding her thinking while she tried to make some sense out of this problem, was Alex Cane.

But how could she turn him away when Jason was so obviously glad to see him?

Katherine owned a simple home, and her living room, though comfortable, was furnished sparsely, with a floral couch and chair, one coffee table, two end tables and a ginger jar lamp. She didn't have a fireplace or Oriental rugs or paintings by world-famous artists. She only had family pictures scattered on all four walls. Yet, Alex Cane didn't seem to mind. In fact, he didn't even seem to notice.

All evening, Katherine watched him as he played with Jason, nodded and made noises of approval to indicate that he heard and understood his bubbly chatter, and in general made Jason the happiest child on the face of the earth, even as he made Katherine comfortable with the idea that he wasn't merely in her home, he appeared to be in her life—maybe even permanently—if only because Jason needed him.

"I know what you're doing," Katherine said as they descended the steps and made their way into her comfortable living room, after putting Jason to bed that night.

"What?" Alex asked innocently.

"You're showing me that we could make a good family."

"So?"

"So it's not going to work."

"Why not?" he asked in exasperation, grabbing her shoulders and spinning her around to face him. "The kid is two... and he needs us. What do you have to do that's so damned important that you can't give him a family?"

Insulted, she lifted her chin. "I'm doing the best I can right now to give him a family."

"Yeah, a family without a dad." He sighed, combed his fingers through his hair, but still kept one hand firmly locked on her shoulder. "Look, Katherine, this is not a lifetime commitment. The way I see this, we have about ten years, eleven at most, before Jason will be telling *us* and a *judge* what he wants done with the rest of his life. Eleven years is not all that long. What are you so damned afraid of?"

Katherine sighed. "I'm not afraid of anything, but I'm not about to break the law, either," she admitted honestly. "What you're asking is that we try to fool a judge into thinking that we've gotten married for all the right reasons, so he'll see us as stable and let us keep our nephew."

"Well, at least you've got that much of it right."

"Oh, I do. I see that quite clearly but I also see two flaws."

"Such as?"

"What makes you so sure Judge Black will give us custody when we get married?"

"Because it makes more sense than sending Jason away. It gives him an easy way out. He almost came right out and told us that's why he warned us about Marissa before the actual hearings started. He *wants* us to come up with an idea that's better for Jason than sending him away."

"Maybe," Katherine agreed quietly.

"So, what's your second problem?"

"Why?"

"Why what?"

"Why are you doing this?"

"To get the chance to raise Jason."

"Too pat," Katherine said and moved away from him. "Too simple. *I* want to raise Jason, too. In fact," she admitted, walking to an end table where she picked up a picture of Jessica, "I promised Jessica that I would."

"And I'm giving you the perfect opportunity."

"No, you're snowballing me. Showering me with superficialities when I'm desperate, so I'll be so overwhelmed with your generosity and kindnesses that I'll agree." She looked at him then. She caught his gaze with her own and wouldn't let him go. Wouldn't let him move. Hoped to keep him so tied up he'd have trouble breathing. After all, it was this look that got her her best contracts. "It's not that simple. Everybody wants something. I'm not budging an inch until I find out what it is you want."

Alex took a minute before he answered her. Katherine watched a vast array of emotions quickly flash across his face, and knew he'd carefully considered everything from lying to baring his soul. When he glanced up at her, though, his face was completely without expression. "You're not going to like this."

"I think I already figured that out."

"All right. The truth is I'm considering expanding my television holdings from two stations to three. And I can't afford to be in a custody battle right now—at least not with Marissa. She's vicious. She'll drag me and my name through the proverbial mud and remind the world that I have a past that doesn't really mix with owning and managing a family station...."

"A *family* station?" she asked incredulously.

He shrugged. "It's where the money is right now," he said, then paced across her living room. "So, are you in or are you out?"

"I think I'll pass," she said and walked to her door, an indication that he should follow her, so she could let him out.

But he wasn't giving up that easily. "Katherine, this isn't just about the station. It's about Jason, too. Damn it, I want to raise Jason, and Marissa's not going to let me have that chance. I can't fight her in court, because I can't beat her at this point."

"And that's really why you want to get married, isn't it? Because you know you can't beat her."

"I didn't get where I am today without understanding the odds, and this one's a loser for both of us. But if we get married, we're the shoo-in, not Marissa, because no rational, logical court in the land would take a child away from his closest two blood relatives. Especially if his closest two blood relatives are married."

"Do you really think it's going to be that easy?" Katherine asked. "That Judge Black will happily accept our marriage and give us Jason without question or comment?"

"Katherine, trust me. We'll be giving Judge Black exactly what he wants. A way to keep Jason right here in Pennsylvania. I'm telling you, he called us in this morning because he was in a jam, looking for an excuse for not sending Jason to live with a family he doesn't know. Our getting married gives Judge Black the perfect reason to keep Jason in his natural home."

"You make it sound so simple."

"It is... it could be. We get married, the judge gives us custody and we raise Jason together. We build the basis of a good strong family, so *Jason* gets what he really needs from us then when Jason is old enough to choose what he wants, we separate, there'll be no custody battle, we'll share. If you want, I'll have my lawyer draw up papers to that effect right now...."

Katherine shook her head in wonder, then pulled her fingers through her hair and walked away from him. "I understand what you're saying," she said, grateful for his honesty about his television station because it was always best to know what you were negotiating with and for. And because in an odd kind of way his greedy reason gave her the first straw to grasp for trusting him. If nothing else, she did know he was being honest. "But this is all happening too fast. Truthfully, Alex, it feels too dishonest."

He shook his head. "It's helping things along, so that they work in our favor."

"I'm not so sure there aren't other options."

"Okay, fine. You think about all this. You think long and hard if that's what you want. I've already admitted I can't beat Marissa alone. I'm coming to you for help and you're refusing. So, in the end, when the judge is sending Jason to Montana, don't come crying to me."

With that he turned and left her house so quickly, Katherine got a spontaneous spasm of shivers. He was right. At this point, if the judge sent Jason away, Katherine would have no one to blame but herself, because Alex Cane had done more than hand her an olive branch.

Katherine arrived at work the next morning wearing a coral suit, white pumps and huge gold hoop earrings. Her fingernails had been painted to match her outfit and her lipstick and blush blended into the color scheme, as well. Her thick auburn hair had been pulled into a tight chignon, with long, lose strands tickling her neck and framing her face.

"Wow! Look at you!" Caryn, Katherine's administrative assistant, said as Katherine walked back down the hall to her office.

"Oh, be quiet."

"Meeting with Mr. Cane today?" Caryn asked sarcastically, but then ruined it by giggling foolishly. Caryn was the only person in Katherine's office who knew about Katherine's custody battle, which meant she was the only person who knew Katherine was fighting with the notorious Alex Cane, and also the only person who knew Katherine absolutely loathed the man.

But Caryn was a romantic, a nineteen-year-old blue-eyed blonde who still believed in all the good things Katherine had forgotten existed in life. So Caryn in her slightly twisted young mind decided Katherine didn't hate Alex Cane; she had a crush on him. Katherine spent fifteen minutes after her custody hearing the day before denying it. But she gave up trying because Caryn didn't seem to be hearing a word Katherine said, and, instead, seemed to be creating some kind of fairy tale out of this whole mess. Because of that, Katherine hadn't told her about the marriage scheme. She didn't dare risk it. Caryn would be writing out invitations and choosing china patterns before Katherine could get it through her head that it was only a marriage of convenience.

"No, I am not meeting with Mr. Cane today. He dropped by the house last night, and I couldn't sleep after he left so I ended up giving myself a manicure."

Caryn was now seated across from Katherine's desk and was listening so intently, Katherine worried Caryn would have a stroke.

"Never mind. It's not important. Anything interesting happen this morning?"

"No," Caryn answered casually, but as she spoke, Denny Maroni, Katherine's boss, poked his head into Katherine's office.

"You," he said, pointing his index finger at Katherine. "In my office. Now."

With that he pulled himself out of her doorway and disappeared down the hall. Katherine swallowed, but

Caryn's eyes grew big with surprise. "I swear, he wasn't supposed to be back until tomorrow."

"Well, he's back now, and I haven't been out of the office to do my job in the last four weeks," Katherine said as she rose from her desk. "So I'd say I'm in trouble." She straightened her suit, though she hadn't been sitting long enough for it to be wrinkled; then, with a regal lift of her head, she exited her office, leaving her stunned administrative assistant behind.

Denny Maroni was one of the new breed of executives who didn't smoke, watched his weight and worked out as much as his busy schedule allowed. As a result, tall, handsome Denny cut quite an impressive figure as he stood behind his massive oak desk, staring out the wall of windows at the back of his enormous, strikingly beautiful office.

When Katherine hesitated by the door, he faced her. "Come in. Come in, Ms. Whitman," he said, motioning with his right arm. "What a pleasant surprise to find you in your office."

Gingerly stepping into the room, Katherine cleared her throat. "I know I shouldn't be spending so much time here in Johnstown, but..."

Denny sighed unexpectedly. "Look, kid—I am not an unsympathetic old man."

Katherine smiled. Denny was forty-two and didn't have a gray strand in his black hair, but he frequently referred to himself as an old man. He was no more an old man than he was an unsympathetic man. However he was a businessman first and foremost, and if Katherine couldn't do her job, Denny's choices were limited.

"I know it has only been a few weeks since your sister died, and, my God, it hurts me to have to bring this up, but we've got a company to run. Tonnage is down in three of our facilities."

She swallowed. "I know."

"I figured a smart girl like you would be watching." Sighing again, he sat on his tall-backed leather chair and said, "I also know you're raising your sister's boy. I'm guessing you're having a little trouble finding a baby-sitter for him when you travel. I'd like to tell you that you can have all the time in the world to work out your problems, but I'm afraid I don't have that luxury. I need to know what you're planning to do."

It crossed her mind to take the easy way out and tell him about Alex Cane's proposal, but then she reminded herself she couldn't do that because it was a ridiculous compromise—although it had actually started to look pretty darn good to Katherine at two o'clock in the morning as she paced her small bedroom.

If she married Alex Cane, Jason would not only be well cared for, he would be well loved. Alex Cane was the first person to make her nephew smile in weeks and right now that wasn't just nice, it was essential. And Katherine wouldn't be giving up custody. She wouldn't even really be sharing it. She would take charge. She would take control. After all, hadn't she handled Alex Cane before, during and after his visit with Jason? With proper supervision Alex could be around and still kept in line.

Even better, Alex Cane's past reputation as being a womanizing scoundrel pointed out clearly that Alex wasn't capable of a real marital relationship—which actually worked in Katherine's favor because there'd be no misunderstanding. There would never, ever be a danger of him falling in love with her, or her falling in love with him. When their time together with Jason ended, they could go their separate ways, no strings attached. She could still have a life. And, selfish though it sounded, the money she would save on room and board during that time would take care of the debt she'd incurred because of Jessica's illness....

Truth be known, in the end, his idea really would give both what they wanted. He would stay out of court even as he won the opportunity to raise his brother's son. She would keep her promise to her sister.

She took a long breath. "I have a couple of options. I only have to choose the best one."

"All right, Katie. Look," Denny said, giving her the direct stare for which he was so famous, "I am not a mean, wicked and evil man."

She smiled. "I know that."

"But we have a new facility coming on-line in December and to my recollection you haven't really started selling it yet."

She shook her head. "No, I haven't."

"I didn't think so," he said, then drew a long breath. "This time next week, somebody's going to be in Ohio promoting that facility. Now, it can be you or it can be somebody I hire, but rest assured, Katie, if I have to hire somebody I have to fire somebody."

She swallowed. "Okay."

"Well, before you capitulate, let me add this. I won't be firing you. I'll be firing Caryn. And you and the new sales rep I hire will be doing all your own paperwork."

She licked suddenly dry lips. "But..."

"No buts. Decisions. I want a decision. If you can't give it to me before you leave today, you'd better have it by nine tomorrow morning."

She took a long breath, let it out slowly, then cleared her throat. "Actually, I don't need any more time."

He looked at her.

"You see... Denny, can you keep a secret?"

His eyes narrowed.

"I, um, you see, pretty soon I'm not going to have to worry about a baby-sitter for Jason and I'll be able to travel all you want because... because I'm getting married."

"What?"

"Well, I'm actually marrying a man who was Jessica's brother-in-law, and he'll be more than happy to care for Jason while I'm on out-of-town trips."

Denny's black eyebrows rose slowly. "Isn't this a little sudden?"

"Well, Alex came into my life... because of my sister's death," she explained, not really lying, merely stretching the truth in a more helpful direction. "And we started seeing each other because of our nephew, and the next thing you know, he asked me to marry him...."

# *Chapter Three*

Once, when Katherine first began working for Penn American Waste Systems, she drove a hundred miles and waited two hours to meet the tallest, angriest man on the face of the earth. He had to have been at least six foot six. If she guessed his weight at three hundred pounds that would have been a conservative estimate. He wore shaggy jeans and a wide belt with a silver buckle in the shape of a trash truck.

Even before she'd opened her briefcase, he rose, leaned across his desk and breathed fire directly into her face. Their company had robbed him blind, their company had stolen his territory, their company couldn't be trusted.

At this moment, standing on Alex Cane's doorstep, ready to ring the bell, Katherine wished she were back at that meeting rather than on the verge of accepting Alex Cane's marriage proposal.

It wasn't bad enough that she didn't want to marry him. It wasn't bad enough that this marriage of convenience felt more like a felony than a viable option for keeping Jason. The worst of it really was, she'd already told Denny that she was getting married and she hadn't yet accepted Alex Cane's proposal. If he'd changed his mind, she was going to be in big trouble. Embarrassed, anyway. If he hadn't, well, that was a whole different kind of trouble. A whole different kind of embarrassment, too.

Drawing a long, deep breath, Katherine lifted her hand to ring the doorbell. The chimes played something Katherine recognized as Mozart, though she couldn't name the actual piece. Then a tall, thin, incredibly well-dressed man answered the door.

She cleared her throat. "I'm looking for Mr. Cane."

The man eyed her critically. "Really?"

Feeling an urge to run, Katherine took a second and composed herself before she said, "My name is Katherine Whitman. I'm..."

"A friend," Alex said from behind the gentleman at the door. Even dressed in navy blue trousers and a simple white shirt open at the neck, he looked spectacular. Sexy somehow, in spite of his modest attire. Katherine supposed it had to be his brilliant green eyes. They were so bright and beautiful, they were mesmerizing.

"I instructed the guard at the gate to let her in. And I'll take it from here, Ronald," Alex directed further. "You may leave."

To Katherine's amazement the tall man bowed at the waist, then simply turned and walked away.

Mouth gaping, Katherine stared at him, but Alex chuckled. "That's Ronald. He runs the estate."

Katherine had been so preoccupied with the weight of her decision that she'd hardly noticed her surroundings as she drove onto Alex's property. But with the use of the word *estate,* Katherine recalled the long, long lane, the security guard who called up to the house to get permission to send her through the gates and the well-manicured grounds that surrounded Alex's huge Tudor mansion.

Now, standing in an echoing foyer, she couldn't stop her eyes from gazing around. The floor looked very much like nearly white marble. A spiral staircase elegantly split the room. Everything—even the tables holding the lamps—was trimmed in gold. The chandelier dripped with elegant crystal.

"You have a lovely home," she managed cautiously, starting out friendly because she didn't want to offend him, and, actually wanted him in a good mood, no matter which way their discussion went.

"Thank you," he said, then motioned for her to walk down a long, dimly lit hallway. "Please, join me in the library."

She nodded and walked down the corridor, her heels tapping on the hard floor. The second she would have reached for the doorknob, Alex was behind her, graciously granting her entrance himself.

"Have a seat," he said. He directed her to a black leather sofa, but rounded a wet bar of black leather and glass. A wooden desk sat in front of a wall of windows, and tall wooden bookcases lined the rest of the room. Every one of them was filled to capacity. A quick glance revealed selections ranging from pop psychology to classic literature, some of the books appearing to be original printings. Black and mauve Oriental rugs accented the hardwood floor. "Would you like a drink?"

She shook her head. "No, I need to be thinking clearly for this discussion."

His eyebrows rose. "Ah, we've got something serious on our minds?"

"As I recall, you asked me to marry you yesterday. I'd think you wouldn't be surprised."

"Actually, I am," he admitted, pouring himself a large glass of orange juice. Katherine noticed he didn't add any alcohol and mentally breathed a sigh of relief. That was a very good sign. "I got the distinct impression you didn't think much of my proposal."

"That was before my boss gave me an ultimatum."

"Really?" he said, his lips winging into a gleeful grin. "What kind of ultimatum?"

She eyed him suspiciously. "You wouldn't by any chance have bribed him into this?"

"I've never had to bribe anyone to do anything. I simply have incredibly good luck, and it looks like it hasn't failed me again."

"Well, if you were really serious about marrying me, then, no, your good luck's in perfect shape."

He set his glass on the bar, braced both his forearms on the glass top and stared at her. "You're agreeing?" he asked, stunned.

"I don't have much choice."

"Wonderful!" he said, but he caught himself and his expression became more sober. "I mean, I'm sorry."

"Oh, you don't have to be sorry," she said, strolling over to the bar. She never had taken a seat on the couch. She'd been so awestruck by the unpretentiousness and warmth of the elegant, obviously expensive room, that she'd been perusing the quarters. "Go ahead and gloat. God knows, I would have gloated had the tables been turned."

Unexpectedly, he broke into unrestrained laughter. "Honesty," he said, then laughed again. "Lord, attractive, hardworking and honest, too. You're going to enhance my image about three hundred percent." And that was really going to work in his favor when it came time to switch the levers to put everything in motion for his new television station. His first motivation for marrying Katherine was and always would be that he needed to keep Jason away from Marissa, but getting a sweet, sensible wife was one hell of an added bonus.

Particularly since she was so darned attractive that no one, absolutely no one, would question why he'd chosen to marry her.

"There is no such thing as three hundred percent," she said sliding onto one of the tall stools.

"Don't go getting all technical on me," he said, and disappeared as he stooped behind the bar. "This calls for champagne."

"I... All right, sure. What the heck."

Alex could tell she almost refused and was glad to see she didn't. He knew this was going to be difficult for her, but sometimes the best way to make a change, particularly such a drastic change, was to just jump right in and do it. Even if it wasn't a real marriage, it had to *look* like a real marriage. They might as well start learning to get along tonight.

He set two fluted glasses on the bar in front of her, then popped the cork of the bottle like a professional.

"You did that as if you're an expert."

He smiled. "I am."

His wonderful smile tripped something in Katherine's chest, and she felt the oddest fluttering. She could have sworn it was her heart, but that was ridiculous. Attractive or not, this man was something akin to her sworn enemy—and she intended to keep it that way. Except where matters pertaining to Jason were concerned.

"I'm not sure I'd brag about it."

"It comes in handy at parties," he announced as if that talent were a diploma from Princeton.

"How lucky for you," she said, then glanced around the room as if seeing it for the first time. Realization after realization poured over her. His money. His reputation. The idea that they would be companions for at least the next *decade.* It was so overwhelming that Katherine almost chickened out. But she thought of Jason, thought of missing him, thought of his crying for her, and she forced her voice to sound calm and casual when she said, "Anything else I should know?"

"I rise early, read for hours, love to walk in the woods and my hobby is horseback riding," he said, but he chuckled, making Katherine feel he wasn't taking this seriously enough.

"That's terrific!" she said, as panic began to well up inside her. They'd made a huge decision, but neither one of them was prepared for it and the whole darned world was going to see right through them. "I'm going to sound like I'm marrying the playboy of the month if I start spouting that to my friends when they ask about my new fiancé. And, believe me, they're going to ask. I'm going to have to face all kinds of questions."

"You?" he said, pouring the frothy liquid into the crystal flutes, finally sounding like a man who was beginning to realize the kind of commitment they were making to each other. "I'm going to have to face the press."

Tipping their glasses forward, they clinked them together in a musical toast. "You *are* the press. Somehow I don't think you're going to have a problem." Even as she said the words, they both raised their gazes away from the meeting glassware and their lines of vision collided. "It's me who's going to have the problem."

*Oh, boy,* she thought, her stomach plummeting to the floor. For the sake of her nephew and a promise to her sister, she was about to commit herself to years with a man she didn't know except by reputation...bad reputation. "Maybe this isn't such a good idea."

"Cold feet?" he asked, then started to laugh.

But his laughter sounded hollow even to his own ears. Good Lord! He'd actually proposed to a woman he didn't know all because he didn't want to fight his sister for his nephew. Was he nuts? Was he stupid? Hell, no, he was desperate. Caught between a rock and a hard place. Ready to launch a television station about the same time he would be fighting his own sister, a sister who'd disowned him, for custody of his only other blood relative. He had to marry this woman. He didn't have any alternative.

He looked at Katherine. She had eyes the color of coffee, soft, pink lips and an incredible body. Every time she moved, he could watch the swell of her breasts as they shifted under the rectangular jacket. Her round derriere gave life to an otherwise straight skirt. Her legs couldn't even be described, they were so perfectly shaped.

And this was the woman he was marrying. Committing himself to for the next eleven years...without benefit of...well, the typical comforts of marriage.

God, was he in trouble.

He would never make it.

Jason spent the following day with Alex and, despite Katherine's apprehension over this whole mess, from the second she said goodbye at Alex's front door she began feeling the weight of burdens being lifted from her back. First, she knew Jason was ecstatic. She did not have to worry about him—not at all, not even a little bit. Second, she knew he would be well cared for.

And third, two minutes after she stepped into her office, she began making appointments with companies in South Carolina, and next week she could work on Ohio. The only problem was, she knew that when she gave Caryn her schedule, Caryn would gleefully ask who would be caring for Jason. Unless Katherine wanted to lie, she would have to admit she was about to marry a man she'd only two days before said she disliked immensely. Because Caryn knew the truth, Caryn was the only possible crack in their story.

That is, once they got a story.

They'd both gotten so nervous the night before, Katherine ended up leaving almost immediately after accepting the proposal, and this morning they not only avoided the topic, they avoided each other's eyes. But Katherine wasn't worried that Alex had changed his mind. One glance at his expressive face when he took Jason from Katherine's arms, and Katherine knew he would visit hell for the chance to keep their nephew. Not that she viewed marrying him that way...

Well, maybe not.

She arrived at Alex's home early that evening and a smiling, jubilant Ronald let her in. "Oh, he was a dickens today, ma'am," Ronald happily reported as he led her down the corridor past the library to a game room. A tall, well-structured man, Ronald looked only slightly silly wearing the huge white apron over his white shirt and dress slacks. "Ran and played as if the estate were made for him. I've never seen Mr. Cane so happy."

Katherine hid her relief. She was pleased that Jason had adjusted, but she'd expected he would. The introduction of Ronald into the situation, a mature adult, a disciplined adult, gave her more than a sense that Jason wouldn't merely run wild, as she feared he would if Alex Cane was his supervisor alone. "Did he have a nap?"

Ronald gave her a quizzical glance. "He told me he didn't want to nap, ma'am," Ronald replied curiously. "I did, however, see to it that he spent an hour of quiet time in the library immediately after lunch." He paused and sent her a meaningful look. "A series of picture books held his attention for much of the time. Even though he didn't nap, he had an hour of quiet time."

Katherine smiled. "And what did Mr. Cane think of this quiet time?"

Ronald turned away from her to open the door, but Katherine suspected that move was prompted by wanting to hide a grin he couldn't seem to contain. "Mr. Cane napped during this time, ma'am."

Katherine burst into unrestrained laughter and that's how she entered the game room. Ronald discreetly closed the door behind her and disappeared as Jason bounced to his feet and ran to her. "Aunt Katie," he cried, throwing himself at her and hugging her around the legs even before she was halfway into the room.

"Hi, Jason," she said, patting his back after she lifted him into her arms. It was wonderful to see him this happy, and to see that she was still a welcome part of his life. But before she could ask him about his day, Katherine heard a muttered, "Damn!" from behind the television.

She tried to peer around the TV. All she saw were the tips of Alex's feet, pointed out from behind the console. "I'd say hello, but it sounds like you're busy," she called.

"Oh, no, I'm not busy," Alex snapped. "I only have a merger agreement sitting on my desk, four faxes I haven't even glanced at yet and two days' worth of mail in my in-basket, but I've got plenty of time to move this VCR...into my library. Exactly where I want it."

Katherine grimaced, still patting Jason's back. "This isn't going to be as easy an arrangement as you'd thought," she pointed out as gently as she could, but facts were facts and this was something they needed to discuss. If the reality of raising a little boy was going to be too much for Alex, now was the time to find out.

"It's not that much of a problem," Alex growled. "Right now, Jason doesn't have a playmate, and he isn't accustomed to the grounds. So we're accommodating him. Once's he's adjusted I'm sure life will go on pretty much as normal for me. Particularly since we're getting another housekeeper, which will free more of Ronald's time to watch over him."

Katherine raised her head. It wasn't a Ward and June Cleaver-style of child care, but it was more than adequate, and from her few conversations with Ronald, Katherine had to admit she liked him. She would entrust Jason to him without qualms.

While Alex set up the VCR, Jason happily chatted about his day. His words were so full of excitement, Katherine's heart filled to bursting. This was it. Jason was really happy.

It wasn't until after dinner, when Ronald had taken Jason outside for a walk that Katherine and Alex actually sat down to discuss their situation. Despite the fact that she was a professional negotiator who knew the value of gradually easing into certain topics, she was also in a horribly unusual situation where *tact* and *diplomacy* were words found only in a dictionary. They had to be blunt, honest and incredibly open with each other because they couldn't be honest with anyone else. If they weren't, if they allowed problems to remain unresolved, or grievances to fester, their marriage would never work out.

In light of all that, Katherine accepted a cup of tea from Alex, and as he sat on the leather chair beside the sofa on which she sat, Katherine said, "You know, of course, that we're probably going to run into some opposition from my parents."

Alex glanced at her. "You mean *you're* going to run into some opposition from your parents."

She shook her head. "*We're,*" she countered. "You're the one who said we have to make this look believable, and it's not going to look believable at all for me to marry someone who refuses to meet my parents."

"Ah, come on, Katherine," he groaned. "I don't get along with anybody's parents."

"I wonder why," Katherine said, but didn't give him a chance to argue or defend himself. "I thought about it this afternoon and realized that despite the fact that my parents aren't going to be thrilled about me marrying you, this might not be so difficult for us to explain. If I told them I needed help caring for Jason and you'd volunteered, that would justify to them why we were spending so much time together and eventually give them a reasonable scenario for how we fell in love."

Alex eyed her suspiciously. "That's not too bad. I think I could work with that."

"Well, that's only the beginning."

"What do you mean 'only the beginning'?"

"We have to give them time, Alex," Katherine explained on a sigh. "Jessica only died last month, they're grieving. I can't suddenly up and marry the man Jessica hated for years. It won't merely seem disloyal, it will almost shout that something's wrong."

She watched Alex settle into the soft folds of his black leather chair as he considered that. He crossed his long legs at the knee and rested his elbow on the chair's arm, even as he rubbed his chin between long, lean fingers.

Today he wore dress slacks and a chambray shirt, again without a tie and unbuttoned at the neck. Though his feet were sockless, he wore neat brown leather loafers and Katherine wondered if he'd spent the entire hot June day dressed like this. Jason had mentioned that they'd been swimming, and given Jason's age, Katherine knew Alex couldn't be a pool-side watcher. He had to be in the water with Jason.

Visions of Alex jumping into a pool also conjured images of him in a bathing suit. She could picture his lean torso glistening in the sun, see his long tan legs... Hot color flared to her cheeks. She stopped her thoughts exactly where they stood because this daydream was getting a little too detailed, a little too easily.

"Okay, the way I see this..." Alex began, glancing over at her. He must have noticed the brightness of her cheeks or eyes because he leaned forward. "Are you okay?"

She cleared her throat. "I'm fine."

"Do you want a glass of water or something? That tea's got to be hot. I can't believe you didn't want a cold drink."

"I rarely drink anything cold. I don't know why. I just don't. Let's concentrate on how we're going to handle my parents."

"Okay. I think what you're telling me is that we need to give your parents the opportunity to see me in a different light, sort of separated from Jessica and her feelings for me."

"Yes. And even then I'm not sure they'll accept this well."

"We can't simply come right out and tell them this is a marriage of convenience?" he asked seriously. "That they don't have to worry about you because we only got married to keep Jason?"

"Oh, yeah, right!" Katherine said sarcastically. "That would be wonderful. There's no way in hell my parents would accept that. They'd offer me money they don't have and then end up blaming themselves for putting me into this position." Realizing arguing wouldn't get them anywhere, she paused, shook her head and then looked directly into his eyes. "Please. The less they know the better."

Alex combed his fingers through his hair. "You'd rather have your parents think you're marrying somebody they don't like, than have them think you'd marry somebody for reasons other than love?" he asked, obviously confused, but at least the conversation was back to being civil.

Katherine shrugged. "Unlike you, they believe in the sanctity of marriage."

"I believe in the sanctity of marriage. I mean, for some people. *Most* people, I guess."

"But not you?"

"Hell, I don't know. I really don't," he said, combing his fingers through his hair again. "Look, what do you say you start dropping hints about how we're taking care of Jason together right now? We'll give them time to get used to me being in the picture and see how it goes. If they don't accept things, we'll think of something then."

His being so perplexed by her wanting to be considerate of her parents seemed to point out that he didn't have anyone to tell, and it made her wonder again about his relationship with Marissa. As far as Katherine knew, relatives were as much of a premium for Alex as they were for her. Yet he had a sister with whom he didn't even speak. How could he dislike his sister so much that he never spoke with her...never saw her?

She debated asking him. It seemed like the perfect opportunity. Then she realized she didn't want to know. It wasn't any of her business. She not only had enough of her own problems, but she didn't want to get involved with his. That would mean she would be getting involved with him. And that would be trouble. At the very least that would complicate things unnecessarily.

She brought the conversation back on track. "So how much time do you think we have before we have to tell the judge we're planning to get married?"

"If we're really good at this, really convincing," he said, "we could let the judge know we're dating next month. That gives us the rest of the summer to *date,* the fall to be engaged and probably means we should get married in early November. Otherwise Judge Black will start to think we're only dating to keep him from making a ruling." He paused, slapped his hands on his thighs. "So it's November. I think we need to get married in November."

The way he analyzed the situation made Katherine laugh.

"What's so funny?" he asked, his eyes narrowing.

"Do you realize how easily we set a date? Most couples argue for months before they come up with a date."

"Yes, well, most couples aren't as fortunate as we are. We have clear-cut goals and responsibilities. We're meeting them."

She liked the way he said that. She wasn't sure why, except to admit that it was a confirmation that he took this as seriously as she did. First, he gave her quarter as far as her parents were concerned. Now he showed her a serious, dedicated side. In spite of some rough spots in the beginning, this discussion was going fairly well.

"I'm getting you a cold drink," Alex insisted suddenly and rose from his seat and bounded to the bar. "It's over ninety degrees out there, and you've been through too much today to confuse your system the way you are." As he said the last, he began to gather bottles from beneath the bar. "This is a very harmless drink. Peach schnapps and orange juice. Some people very vulgarly call it a Fuzzy Navel," he said, his tone so serious, Katherine chuckled. "But I'm trying to impress you, so we'll call it peach schnapps and orange juice."

Shaking her head, she took the glass from his hand, then slid onto a bar stool. "You don't have to be so proper around me. In fact, I like you better when you're angry and frustrated because at least then I get a clear picture what I'm getting myself into."

"Scared?" he asked quietly, his gaze searching her eyes.

She drew a long breath and realized she desperately needed to confide in someone, and he was the only one with whom she could speak honestly about this. "Of course I'm scared. You're trying to keep up the pretense of being polite and wonderful, but someday we're going to run into something we can't compromise on, and I'd like to get a gauge for your temper. Your *real* temper."

He leaned across the bar. "Actually, I don't have a temper."

She rolled her eyes heavenward. "Everybody has a temper."

"Not me. If something goes wrong, I never think of it as a mistake or problem, but actually life's way of pointing you in another direction. I look at problems like surprises. Gifts from fate."

"And that's what you think this is?" she asked, indicating their predicament and their decision to marry.

When he grinned, the lines around his eyes deepened, giving him a more mature look. For the first time since she met him, he looked all of his thirty-six years.

"Actually, yes. Your presence in my life solves a lot of problems. Marrying a career woman who has both feet on the ground will clean up my image so well and so quickly, it will be as if I never had one. I'm taking full advantage of that for my new station."

"How lucky for you."

"You don't know the half of it," he said as he shifted his elbow on the bar and brought his face to within inches of hers. "I also enjoy being in the company of pretty women, and I think you're incredibly beautiful."

His comment didn't surprise her in the slightest, except that she reacted to it. A pulse point in the middle of her stomach jumped. She didn't even know she had a pulse point in her stomach, let alone know what it meant when that particular point suddenly became active. She did, however, suspect it wasn't good.

Sliding off the stool, she said, "Now I can see I haven't been waiting for you to lose your temper. *This* is the other shoe I've been waiting to drop."

"Why?" he asked, rounding the bar, following her though she'd wanted to pace and now she couldn't. It almost seemed he was trying to trap her, corner her.

"Don't you like me?"

She looked at him as if he were crazy. "You can't be serious."

"What? You don't even want to try?"

"Try what?" she asked.

"Try to have a real marriage."

Her mouth dropped open. "That wasn't the deal."

"As I recall, we don't really have a deal."

She found herself backing away from him, and only then realized he was advancing on her. Fear settled in the pit of her stomach, but with it came a set of butterflies and a sense of anticipation that no wise woman would have entertained with the likes of this man.

"Then I think it's time we created one."

"Okay," he agreed. He stopped and Katherine knew that was because he'd more or less cornered her. Her stomach fluttered again, but she drew a long, quieting breath. She'd handled bigger, badder, tougher men than him.

"First," she said calmly, rationally, "get it straight that this is a marriage of convenience. Nothing more."

New light twinkled in his green eyes. "You're so sure about that. How do you know I don't genuinely believe this marriage is for real?"

"The only way a marriage is real is when two people love each other. And don't try to feed me any bull about loving me. You don't even know me," she succinctly reminded him. "We met three days ago."

"Wrong. We met at Ryan and Jessica's wedding. And though I obviously didn't make very much of an impression on you since you don't remember that, you did make an impression on me. Even at eighteen, I thought you were a knockout. How do you know I haven't been carrying a torch for *you* since then?"

The absurdity of it caused her mouth to fall open again and she burst into relieved laughter. "You're an animal, you know that? A complete fool. If that's the best you've got, thank you for using it because you just convinced me that I don't have a damned thing to worry about."

"Oh really," he said before he bent his head and kissed her.

# Chapter Four

His lips were warm and wet, the kiss as soft as a whisper in a dark room.

But Katherine felt it the whole way down to her toes. The light pressure of his mouth against hers was more than a kiss, it was an expression of something she couldn't quite understand. Given their proximity, and the fact that she was securely trapped between a wall and the arm of the sofa, he could have forced her. He did not. He could have nuzzled and suckled and tantalized her. He did not. The breath of a movement of his lips across her lips was nothing more than a question, a suggestion.

And her reaction to it was even more puzzling. Every nerve ending in her body sprang to life. Desire hit her so quickly and unexpectedly, she didn't have a chance to stop it. For all her declarations of dislike for this man, her body never seemed to have been paying attention.

She took the available half step backward and effectively broke the contact. Yet another confirmation. He was asking, maybe suggesting, but the decision was hers.

"No," she said quietly, then shook her head for emphasis. "I want this to be strictly business. Impersonal."

*Impersonal?* he thought. He had absolutely no idea of why. Not when they could share breath-stopping, earth-shaking kisses like that. If that wasn't proof positive they were more than capable of having a real relationship, Alex didn't know what was.

But one look in her cool brown eyes told Alex he was losing it. He might have been affected by that kiss, but she, quite obviously, had not been. And that bothered the hell out of him.

Salvaging his pride and his dignity as best he could, and taking control of this situation while he still had the chance, Alex said, "Fine. Whatever. I just think we're missing out on a really great opportunity here."

He turned away casually, so casually, Katherine could have been offended were it not for the idea that she wanted him to turn away. Her eyes narrowed. "Little bit of an egotist, aren't we?"

"Since you might have taken that as a compliment," he said, pivoting to face her suddenly, "I'm beginning to think it's your ego that needs work, not mine." He swung away again and walked to the French doors behind the desk. "I'll get Jason for you."

He returned to the library with Jason perched on one shoulder. To Katherine, he looked a little too happy for a man who'd quarreled with her two minutes ago, and that in and of itself ignited her anger again—which was ridiculous. She really didn't have to fight with this man. She didn't want him to like kissing her. She didn't care that he turned away casually. He was *supposed* to want to spend more time with Jason than he spent with her, anyway.

"Here you go, sport," he said, sliding Jason to the floor. "I'll see you in the morning."

"Okay," Jason happily agreed, accepting a hug from his uncle.

Katherine gratefully turned to leave the room with her nephew, but as she did Alex caught her arm. "Wait, let Ronald help him get his things. I think we need to talk for another second."

A nerve jumped in her neck, but she only nodded her agreement, glad he was about to apologize for kissing her so that their relationship could go back to normal again. Instead, the minute Jason and Ronald left the room, he asked her if he could take Jason shopping the next day.

Katherine stared at him. "Excuse me?"

He sighed. "I'd like to buy Jason some new things. Not that there's anything wrong with his present things," he hastily assured her. "But I'd like to have enough clothing here that we wouldn't ever have to pack overnight bags or run to your house every time we change our plans. That's such a damned nuisance and it precludes us from doing things spontaneously."

Katherine merely continued to gape at him. He wasn't going to apologize for that kiss. She still felt that she had a right to slap his face for kissing her. Yet, there he stood casually talking about their nephew.

"That's fine," she said, and lifted her chin defiantly, even as she plastered a big smile on her face. "It's a wonderful idea."

She left with her head high and proud, wondering why the hell she felt as disappointed as a teenager who thought she was going to be asked to the prom by the captain of the football team only to discover all he wanted was her best friend's phone number.

* * *

Alex called her at the office the next day. Still stinging, Katherine spoke politely, but without much friendliness. Yet Alex didn't seem to mind. In fact, he didn't seem to notice. He wanted to take Jason to New York. Which meant he wanted to keep him overnight. She knew a minute of discomfort, a minute of doubt; then he told her Ronald would be accompanying them. At that moment Denny stepped into the room waving a contract, and Katherine decided to let them go.

"When can I tell people about this wedding thing?" Denny asked anxiously, as he took a seat across from her desk. "I'm about to burst. Good God, Katherine, you're marrying a celebrity, and you'd think you were on your way to the electric chair."

His observation caught her off guard, but also clued her in to something very important. People would soon be watching her.

Knowing this, she laughed airily, trying to lighten the mood. "Sorry. It's just that Alex is leaving for a few days and I guess I'm not handling it well."

"You are such a surprise," Denny said, then shook his head as he rose from his seat. "But don't expect me to keep this secret long," he advised honestly. "I never was good with things like this."

"I won't," Katherine assured her boss. "We need to...want some privacy," she decided at the last second, finally thinking of an excuse that would strike a chord with Denny. "We want some privacy as a family before all this hits the press and they start hounding us."

"Oh," Denny said, understanding. "Yeah, I guess you're right."

* * *

Though she'd thought of the perfect alibi, Katherine told Alex the story when he and Jason returned on Friday evening. He pondered the situation for only a second before he said, "Your boss accidentally stumbled onto something we should have thought of before."

"What's that?" Katherine asked.

"I'm a public-eye person, Katherine," Alex said seriously as he fell into the leather chair beside the couch. "And when you marry me, you will become a public-eye person, as well."

She took a long breath. "I'm beginning to realize that."

"You can back out."

"No," she said, and shook her head. "Jason's too happy."

"And you?"

"Actually, the situation relieves so many burdens, a little publicity doesn't scare me all that much."

Her answer didn't please him. It appeared that she understood her own end of the bargain, but she didn't grasp yet how much *he'd* placed on the roulette table and how much he stood to lose. He'd gambled everything he had on this third station, figuring he would take his public licks for his past, and still get by. But arranging a fake marriage to snag his nephew might be considered a little too much for even the most forgiving of public eyes. It would be no better than fighting his sister in court. The only advantage was that in this scenario he could keep Jason.

The easiest way to prevent a public disaster would be for them to really explore the possibility of a relationship. Then their kisses would be packed with curiosity and emotion, and their fights—when they had them—would be real, believable...explainable. Besides, that kiss wasn't completely one-sided. He would swear she felt something when he kissed her. Now all he had to do was get her to admit it.

He sprang from his seat and sat beside her on the sofa. "Pay attention to this and pay attention closely because I don't ever want to repeat it."

His voice was so serious, Katherine swallowed. Not from fear of Alex, but from some odd, unexplainable sensation that juxtaposed trepidation over their situation with dreaded excitement over his proximity.

"This marriage can cost me a great many things."

She drew a long breath and set her mind on ignoring the strong, lean body beside her. "I thought you said this marriage would give you a great many things."

"If we convince everyone we're legit, it will. If we don't, or if we look unhappily married, my life—*our* lives—will turn into a nightmare. There's nothing more tempting to the press than an unhappily married couple. But there's also nothing so boring to the press as a happily married couple. So we can't just be married, Katherine. We've got to make it look like we're happy. Actually planning to spend the rest of our lives together. Or else we'll be hounded by the press so much, the judge won't merely take Jason from us, other courts won't consider our appeals seriously."

She frowned. "I hadn't thought of that."

"So you might as well prepare yourself for the fact that I'm going to kiss you in public. Not often, not hard, not embarrassingly. But I am going to kiss you, and unless you can figure out a way to pretend you like it, you're going to ruin this whole charade."

*Pretend she liked it!* She almost laughed. Her toes had only uncurled this morning from a kiss that happened two days ago. "I'll be more careful," she said docily.

The long breath he drew amply voiced his dissatisfaction. "That's all you have to say?"

She shrugged. "I'm sorry. This whole situation is new to me. It's going to take me a while to get used to everything." She brightened and glanced up at him. He was watching her hopefully. "So there's another reason to give ourselves a few weeks before we announce this. Especially to the judge."

"Yeah, right," he said, disappointed again, and rose from the sofa.

"You do realize that our first order of business is to be seen in public?" he asked as he strode to the bar.

She nodded. "I thought we'd go somewhere with Jason."

"Sounds good," he agreed, inclining his head, and unexpectedly Katherine noticed how the early-evening sunlight seemed to glisten around him. He had an aura, a presence, and it wasn't merely a power or money thing. There was something completely sexual and primitive about him, and wrapping it up in sophisticated clothing didn't hide it. If anything, it seemed to magnify the way that he tingled with sexual electricity.

"How about if we go to an amusement park next weekend?"

"Fine," she said absently, suddenly anxious to get away from him. Not only was she feeling the desire to let herself be attracted to him, but she hated it when discussions that would otherwise be personal took on such an air of business. For the first time she realized she'd reduced her personal life to a business arrangement, and she just now realized that she wouldn't have a personal life anymore.

Her entire life was a business arrangement, with no hope for escape. It was a crushing, brutal realization.

She glanced at Alex again. He was leaning against the bar, looking like every woman's fantasy. She wasn't so stupid that she didn't realize Alex's odd disappointment this evening actually stemmed from the belief they should try to have a real marriage. This marriage did more for him than give him the opportunity to raise Jason, and because of that he would happily give it an honest try. And he was attracted to her. His verbal declaration may have sounded like a line, but his eyes were more honest than his words. He found her attractive.

She found him attractive.

Lord, it would be so easy...

Swallowing, she rose from the couch. "Let's get Jason," she croaked, then cleared her throat. "I mean, I think it's time for me to go."

Alex smiled knowingly. "Do you always run away from the obvious?"

His arrogance saved her. So, he'd figured out that she was attracted to him. Some surprise. Every woman in the world was attracted to him. The only difference was, she had no intention of becoming one of his conquests. And that's what she would be. Just another woman who couldn't resist him. Well, she *could* resist him. Any woman with an ounce of self-respect could see right through his lines. "No. I simply run away from the stupid." She snagged her clutch bag from the sofa and walked toward the French doors. "Let's get Jason."

The trip to the amusement park went well. No one seemed to recognize Alex. True, he wore dark glasses and cutoff blue jeans, but he was still Alex Cane. Katherine thought surely someone, anyone, would notice him. But no one did. The day became a quiet, peaceful interlude of family fun. Jason even rode the kiddie water slide without incident.

The following weekend they went to a state park. They hiked; they swam in a lake; they took out Alex's boat. Again, no one seemed to notice or care who he was. Unexpectedly, with the wind whipping through her hair as the boat careened through the water, Katherine realized she was becoming very comfortable with this arrangement. So was Alex. And Jason was beaming. Maybe this wouldn't be so hard. After all, Alex was a business legend, not a rock star. Not a TV star. Not someone people recognized at first glance—or cared about, if they recognized him on their second glance.

Completely relaxed, Katherine didn't protest when Alex slid his arm around her waist as they walked back to his Bronco. It was night now, the small boat was secured on its trailer and they were ready to drive home. Jason was already half-asleep as they placed him in his car seat.

"Nice day," she said quietly as Alex guided her to the passenger door.

"Very nice," he agreed softly. "If nothing else, we're going to make Jason very happy."

"I don't think we're going to be all that unhappy in the process," she said, but she laughed. "You love all this."

"I adore all this," he admitted, then turned her around in his arms. He leaned against the car door and let his arms, which were looped around her waist, drop to the small of her back.

"I think that's because you're discovering you're going to be a wonderful father."

He inclined his head. "Four years ago you wouldn't have been able to say that. Six months ago you wouldn't have been able to say that. But today...yeah. I think I'm going to do okay for Jason."

"That's good," she said, smiling up at him. The light breeze slid beneath her hair and raised it, only enough to cool her neck and remind them of where they were. Bright stars twinkled in a black sky. The scent of the water wafted over them. "This means a lot to you, doesn't it?"

"Very, very much," he said, staring at her with the oddest expression. "Actually, much more than I thought when I suggested the deal."

Though his arms were wrapped around her and resting close to an intimate part of her body, they really weren't touching otherwise. Yet, the moment itself, the darkness, the intense beauty of the lake lent an intimacy to the pose that went beyond what either intended. They were two people trying to give the public the impression that they were falling in love, but right now there wasn't another soul within two hundred feet.

"Well, I guess we'd better go," Katherine suggested softly.

"Okay," he agreed, but rather than breaking the contact, he leaned the few millimeters necessary to brush his lips across hers. The whisper of his breath fanned her face in the last seconds before their mouths met, so she could have stopped him, could have even turned her head slightly to prevent contact, but, mesmerized by the mood and the moment, she shifted enough that her mouth met his.

As he increased the intensity of the kiss, so did she. When he twisted, she followed. And while he tightened his hold on her waist, she raised her hands to his shoulders. All in all, it felt like something akin to a perfectly choreographed dance routine. Until she realized what was happening. They weren't pretending. They were really kissing. And she liked it.

## *Chapter Five*

Katherine's moist, dewy lips felt the chill immediately as Alex pulled away from her. Slightly disoriented, she blinked up at him. Every nerve ending in her body hummed with anticipation, even as the blood in her limbs seemed to have turned to slow-moving lava.

Without thinking of consequences, Katherine drew a long breath to recover at least a part of her senses. The move seemed to confuse him. He tilted his head in question, and Katherine watched the moonlight play over his alarmingly handsome face.

His vivid green eyes shone as clearly and brightly as the glistening lake in the light of the full moon. His smooth skin had acquired a deeper, more even shade of color from the day in the sun, highlighting his strong-boned features in such a way as to make his face more attractive than it already was. His sandy hair skimmed his forehead and, for a second, Katherine felt the urge to touch it, to see if it was as soft and silky as it looked.

He surprised her then by brushing his thumb across her lower lip. The blood in her limbs absolutely stopped, causing her knees to feel as weak and wiggly as warm gelatin. The expression in his eyes called to her, called to some instinctive part of her in such a way that it was as frightening as it was compelling and arousing.

But she realized that was because she was being pulled in by the expression on his face, the mesmerizing effects of his piercing, yet somehow gentle gaze. She had to stop falling under his spell. Not only was he *the* master when it came to getting his own way, particularly with women, but he wasn't affected, only affecting. Jessica had told her story after story of how Alex manipulated women. She'd told her stories of the different women Alex had in his life, and how Alex had bragged that he couldn't be faithful. This wasn't the kind of man you committed to for life, because *he* couldn't commit for life. And no wise woman should be so naive as to think *her* love could change him.

Still, Katherine didn't say a word, didn't move. Alex opened his mouth slightly, as if he were about to say something, but he quickly snapped his mouth closed and shook his head as if to clear a haze. Undoubtedly, he'd just reminded himself that no matter how seductive the night or the kiss, he really didn't want to be tied down any more than she wanted to tie him down. They had made an arrangement for Jason's sake, that was all. They had to remember that.

"We'd better get going," he said, attempting a light, airy tone, but he failed miserably. His voice came out as a low, seductive whisper.

Katherine licked her dry lips. "Yes," she said, feeling an enormous sense of relief as he stepped away from her. It was unbelievable that two intelligent people could let the pull of primitive attraction tamper with their ability to think, but facts were facts. Fighting chemistry and animal instinct wasn't nearly as easy as some people thought. "I do have work in the morning."

But Alex wasn't as concerned about the chemistry as he was about the fact that he was beginning to like her. Really like her. Dammit, he even liked the fact that she didn't want to get involved with him. Strange as it sounded, it showed how much common sense she had. He jumped into the Bronco and slammed the door behind him.

*That* he'd have to think about.

Neither said a word on the drive home. Alex only broke the silence after he turned off the ignition. "I wish you'd reconsider letting Jason stay overnight with me."

She shook her head. "This situation is supposed to look as if it happened slowly, almost accidentally." She risked a look at him. "You're pushing."

He smiled and even in the dark car, his white teeth gleamed brightly. "It's my trademark."

"Well, save it," she said, and opened her car door.

He followed suit, then moved to the back of the Bronco where he lifted Jason from his resting place without waking him. Katherine opened her front door, indicated with a motion of her hand that Alex could precede her into the house and up the steps to Jason's room. When Alex came downstairs, Katherine already had all of her picnic supplies from the Bronco, so that there was no reason for him to delay.

He cleared his throat. "Well, I'll be going, then."

"Okay. I'm very tired and really need some sleep tonight."

"We had quite a day."

"Yes, we did," she agreed, but with a note in her voice that indicated that she didn't wish to reminisce about it.

He sighed. "Okay, I'm going," he said, turned toward the door, then faced her again. "If you really don't want this relationship to turn into more than you bargained for," he said lightly, "try not to look so cute in a bathing suit next time."

Katherine frowned at him because it was an old line, but the look he gave her before he turned to walk out the door was almost a warning.

But he needn't have gone to the trouble of warning her off because on the drive home from the lake a litany of Jessica's words and cautionings had rolled through her brain, reminding her that Alex couldn't be trusted, shouldn't be trusted.

He was trouble.

He was problems.

He was pain.

Katherine crawled into bed, knowing she had absolutely nothing to worry about. Jessica would never let her fall in love with him.

The next morning when Katherine pushed through the door of the building that housed the regional office of Penn American Waste Systems, her eyes grew huge with surprise. Waiting for the elevator, chatting like two polite strangers were Denny and Judge Arnold Black.

She stopped inside the main entrance. The last person she wanted to "run into" was Judge Black, but Johnstown was a small city and "running into" people was a very common occurrence. Still, she knew that if she lingered a few seconds by the building's door she would miss the elevator and the confrontation. She debated the possibility that she should walk over to make sure Denny didn't mention something to the judge about her engagement, then realized her engagement wouldn't even enter Denny's mind, unless she walked over.

Just as she expected, the elevator bell sounded and the judge entered without seeing her, but as Denny turned to step into the car, he spotted her.

"Come on, Katherine," he called jovially. "Hurry it up and we'll wait for you."

Since she didn't have an excuse for wanting to stay in an empty lobby, Katherine had no choice but to join her boss and Judge Black in the elevator. She nodded a greeting to Denny as she entered, then turned and said hello to the judge.

"Katherine," the judge said in response as Katherine turned to face the elevator doors. "What are you doing here?"

"Penn American has their regional office in this building," Katherine answered noncommittally.

"Oh," Judge Black said. The silence stretched between them for a few seconds, then he added, "My son's law firm is in this building."

"That's nice," Katherine said, wishing the elevator would move more quickly. Any second now, the judge could mention her custody dispute with Alex, albeit only as a polite inquiry to make conversation. If he did, Denny would easily put two and two together about her sudden engagement.

She glanced up. The floor indicator said they'd only hit the third floor. Unable to stop herself, Katherine asked, "What floor is your son's office on?"

"Fifteen," he replied.

The indicator moved to four. Katherine swallowed. "Oh."

"Normally, I wouldn't show my face in his building," the judge admitted with a chuckle. "Arnold, Jr., doesn't like his father interfering in his practice, particularly since I'm a judge and he's concerned about propriety. But he's handling some property transactions for his mother and me so he's going to be seeing a lot more of me than he wants to see over the next few weeks."

"The next few weeks?" Katherine asked, her mind calculating the possibility that Denny and Judge Black could run into each other often if Judge Black came into this building several times for the next few weeks. One of those times, either one of them or both of them could inadvertently slip the name Alex Cane. Which meant the possibility existed that either one of them, or both of them, could eventually figure out that Katherine's upcoming marriage was nothing but a strategy to fool the judge into letting her and Alex keep Jason.

Denny glanced from the judge to Katherine. "You two know each other?" he asked curiously.

Katherine waited for Judge Black to answer, but recognizing that Katherine knew Denny better than he did, Katherine supposed the judge deferred to her.

"Yes," she said carefully. "Judge Black is presiding over Jason's custody case."

"There's a case?" Denny asked.

"Well, yes," the judge answered, surprised. "When the court gets more than one petition for custody of the same child, there's always a hearing."

"A hearing?" Denny asked, arching a brow in Katherine's direction. "I didn't know about this."

"And this is my floor," the judge announced, happy to slip out of the discussion which, for Judge Black, had unexpectedly turned awkward. "Katherine, it was nice to see you again. I hope you're getting everything straightened out."

"Oh, she is," Denny said, seemingly recovering his memory about Katherine's problems of a few weeks before, and obviously thinking that the problem to which the judge referred was overnight care for Jason. "She's..."

The elevator door closed as Denny said, "Getting married."

Katherine just barely stopped her legs from buckling under her. Alex would have killed her if she'd let the cat out of the bag prematurely.

"So that's why you've speeded things up," Denny said as he motioned for her to precede him out of the elevator when it reached their floor.

"Speeded things up?" she asked cautiously.

"Well, you know. Did you hurry your wedding plans so you'd have a husband so you wouldn't lose Jason?"

"Actually, Denny," Katherine answered slowly, laying her hand on his forearm to stop him when he would have opened the glass door into their office, "that *is* sort of part of it."

"But?" he asked perceptively.

She sighed. "But we're not getting married exclusively so that I'll retain custody of Jason," Katherine explained, desperately trying to keep most of their story intact, and realizing that as she did so she was out-and-out lying. Her face flamed with color, and she wished futilely that she were anywhere, doing anything, other than lying to a man she greatly admired.

"Well, I know that," Denny replied indignantly. "Give me some credit here, Katherine." Seeing Katherine's discomfort, he stopped, blew his breath out on a sigh. "Okay, so you're speeding things up a bit. What's the harm? You and your guy would have gotten married anyway, right?"

Big-eyed, Katherine only stared at him.

"Who am I, or who is anybody else for that matter, to be judgmental about the way you're pushing the date up a little bit?"

Katherine swallowed, realizing that Denny hadn't figured out that Alex was one of the other petitioners in Jason's case, and realizing that he was making assumptions that were dead wrong, but which—to Denny—were perfectly acceptable.

"I'm behind you all the way, kid," he added, and turned to open the door, but changed his mind and faced her again. "And believe me, if I see the judge, there'll be no more discussions about you and your custody case. I won't mess this up for you."

When Katherine arrived at Alex's house that night, she gave Jason a hug, got a behavior report from Ronald, then made her way to Alex's office. Ronald took Jason upstairs to clean him up before she took him home.

She tapped twice on Alex's office door then simply pushed it open and entered.

"Hey, stranger," he said, looking up from his reading. He wore brown tortoiseshell glasses, and instead of them making him look overly studious, they somehow managed to make him look sexy.

Images of kissing him flooded through her, weakening her limbs, but other more pressing concerns pushed them aside. "We have a problem."

"I figured that when I got the message that I was to have Ronald keep Jason occupied so we could have a discussion when you got home," he said, gesturing for her to take the seat in front of his huge mahogany desk. "What's up?"

"Judge Black's son has an office in Penn American's building."

"So?" Alex asked, but there was laughter in his voice and in his eyes.

Katherine sighed. "So, Arnold, Jr.'s handling a property transaction for the judge and the judge is going to be in and out of our building a great deal for the next several weeks."

"So?"

"So, Denny, my boss was in the elevator with me and the judge this morning. To explain how the judge and I know each other I had to tell Denny about the hearing. Now Denny thinks we moved the date of our wedding up in order to keep custody of Jason."

"You told the judge about the wedding?" Alex asked, as he tapped a pencil on his desk, his brow furrowed in concentration.

"No. Denny drew most of his conclusions after the judge got off for his floor."

"So where's the problem?"

"Denny has no idea that you're one of the other petitioners for custody of Jason. He thinks that other people are trying to take Jason from you and me and because of that we're getting married. Or, as he put it, we pushed up the date of our wedding."

"That's damned close to the truth."

"Too close. Denny swears he's not going to talk to the judge about this anymore, but I know Denny. He's got a heart of solid gold, and if he thinks it will help our cause to put in a good word, that's exactly what he'll do. And if he does, he's going to blow our plan."

Alex tapped the pencil for a few minutes, then said, "Okay, you'll have to start arriving and leaving at the same time your boss does to make sure that he doesn't say anything out of line."

Katherine shook her head. "That's not practical."

"Okay, then we go in the opposite direction."

"The opposite direction?"

"It's time to come out of the closet, Katherine. We've already had three dates with Jason. It's time to take our relationship one step further."

"But—"

"No buts. It's the only thing to do. We have to start doing things together, just you and me, so that people begin to see us as a couple, not caretakers."

"Nobody except your staff and your visitors has ever seen us together as caretakers," Katherine protested. "We never saw anybody when we took Jason out. We can't all of a sudden start dating...."

"Katherine, this is not all of a sudden. We've virtually kept constant company for the last three weeks. We have a story. We have our alibis. It's time to bring them out to the public."

Katherine sighed. Panic gave her goose bumps. Not because she wasn't ready to announce that they were dating, but because she knew the announcement meant they would actually have to date. And actually dating meant that they really would become part of each other's lives. She'd worked very hard to integrate herself into his as inconspicuously as possible. But there was no guarantee that he'd return the favor. He was brass, bold and unexplainably arrogant sometimes. Not only could she not be sure her friends and co-workers would accept him, but she couldn't be sure he wouldn't alienate the few friends she made in the very scarce spare time she'd had while juggling her job and caring for her sister.

Her mouth dropped open at the very thought that she might lose her precious few friends because of him. "I can't. Not this quickly, not this way."

He stopped her tirade with a wave of his hand. "Then what do you suggest?"

"That we spend a little more time in public with Jason."

Exasperated, Alex ran his hand down his face. "We've spent three weeks with Jason."

"But not in front of people who count."

"People who count?" he asked skeptically.

"Friends, co-workers, neighbors. You know, we've never even run into one of my neighbors when we were out on the lake or at the amusement park."

"Katherine, you can't have everything. We're running out of time. In a few weeks, we've got to go to the judge and explain that we're dating. We can't do that unless we're actually dating."

"I know," Katherine agreed, sensing that he was weakening. "But do one favor for me. Come into the office with Jason. Do it under the pretense of showing him where I work. I'll introduce you around as Jason's uncle, everyone will get used to you and then we'll date."

Sighing, he shook his head. "We don't really have the time."

But she needed the time, if only to get the security of the confirmation that marrying Alex wouldn't cost her real friendships. She didn't think she could back out of her commitment to him and to Jason if the cost of this relationship would be that dear, but at least she wanted to keep her options open. "Please?"

She wasn't sure if it was her use of the word *please,* or her submissive tone of voice, but one of the two caused his brows to raise. And also caused him to relent. "Okay. But only because that fits with the story that caring for Jason brought us together, and only if I can make this *visit* tomorrow."

"Tomorrow?"

"We're running out of time, Katherine."

On a long sigh, Katherine nodded her agreement.

"Okay, now, one more question. What happens if *I* run into the judge in the elevator?"

"You tell him you're bringing Jason in to show him where I go everyday when I leave him with you, to go to work. Make it look like Jason misses me when I'm gone, or wonders where I am, and we're trying to alleviate his fears," she said, then paused to think the scenario through. "Actually, running into the judge might work in our favor. It could make it look like we're already functioning as a team."

"Yeah, that's true. All right, princess, you've got your extra few days," Alex said, and finally smiled at her. Katherine's heart stopped, then sped up in response to the mere expression on his face. Until that very second, she hadn't realized how important it was to her that she be able to have some say in their relationship. Not merely a say, but some power. He was, after all, a very powerful man, not a man used to doing anyone else's bidding. Imagining spending the rest of her life with someone who didn't know how to compromise was like imagining spending the rest of your life in prison.

"But I'm still partial to getting it all out in the open as soon as we can. I'd also suggest that we visit the judge almost immediately after I visit your office."

"Immediately?" she asked incredulously. "As in tomorrow afternoon?"

"Well, no," Alex said. "But soon. Within the week."

He waited for her to reply, but when she only licked her lips, he added, "Compromise, Katherine. I gave you a concession, now you return the favor."

Katherine drew a long breath. "All right."

"All right, we'll tell the judge next week?" he prodded when she didn't elaborate.

"Yes, we'll tell the judge next week," she said, but in her head she was already wondering if there wasn't a way around that. She almost wished Alex would run into Judge Black in her building's elevator because that seemed like the perfect way to introduce the judge to their relationship. It would look phony to make an appointment with him and tell him they were dating. Yet when Alex explained the rationale behind his decision to meet the judge in his office, Katherine had to admit she agreed. The judge wouldn't have any way of knowing they were dating unless they told him. And trying to set up a situation wherein the judge saw them together in public would probably end up looking even more phoney than approaching him directly.

"Can I get you something to drink?" Alex asked casually when their business conversation ground to a halt.

"No. If you'll excuse me, Jason and I need to go home."

As was his practice, Alex didn't argue when Katherine decided to take Jason and go home. Katherine rose from her seat and began walking to the door, but she stopped and faced him again. "Denny, my boss, is a very nice, very sweet man who's been nothing but good to me. When you come into the office, I want you to be nice to him. I want you to be nice to everybody. They're like family to me."

Her serious admission wasn't easy for her, because they both knew that people without actual blood relatives relied more heavily on the kindnesses of their friends than normal people did. But for every bit as much as it would have hurt Katherine for him to argue with her, it would have also caused a strange pain if he would have sympathized.

After an uncomfortable moment of silence, Alex grinned. "Katherine, when have I ever not been nice?"

Relieved that he'd taken the discussion into territory both could handle easily, she reached for the doorknob. "Let's not forget, your reputation precedes you."

With that she walked out of the door, gathered Jason and his things and made her way home.

She slept soundly that night, peacefully and deeply, despite the fact that her life was no longer in her hands, but in the hands of a man she hardly knew. How he treated her friends and co-workers was every bit as important as how he treated her family. It would reflect back on her as completely as if he really were her husband, or her fiancé because soon that's what everybody would think he really was. He could, with a few callous words, affect her working relationship, her job, her relationship with her parents.

She had to trust that he wouldn't.

The next morning, she dressed carefully. Cobalt blue dress. White pumps. Pearls. When Alex arrived, with Jason clinging to his neck as if frightened out of his mind, Katherine glided into the reception room, smiled brilliantly at Alex when she said hello, then turned her full attention to Jason. She comforted him about her office surroundings, impressing upon him that they weren't scary because they were quiet, and when she would have taken him back down the hall to introduce Jason to her boss and her administrative assistant, and by association introduce Alex, Denny came bursting into the reception area.

"My God! Alex Cane!" he boomed, striding over to offer his hand to Alex. "What a pleasure."

"The pleasure is mine," Alex replied, and Katherine realized she'd worried for nothing. Wasn't he the man who'd built his companies on the basis of his handshake and his smile? "Katherine talks about you all the time."

"Really?" Denny said, raising his eyebrow as he looked at Katherine. "What does she say?"

"Confidentially," Alex confessed, his voice dropping to a stage whisper, "she's told me you're the best boss she's ever had."

Denny laughed exuberantly. "I am," he agreed, but the phone rang and the receptionist told Denny it was the corporate office. Denny strode down the hall, on to business, without a backward glance.

"You passed one," Katherine whispered to Alex, then looked down at Jason. "I want you to see where Aunt Katherine goes everyday when she leaves you, so you understand what I do."

Not quite interested, Jason nodded anyway.

"This would work a lot better if we could get the kid to drum up some enthusiasm," Alex whispered as they walked down the hall to her office.

"He's doing fine," Katherine insisted. "Remember, this visit's supposed to ease my guilty conscience for leaving him every day. A little rebellion from him could actually help our cause."

Jason rebelled beautifully. About two seconds before they reached her office door, he stopped dead in his tracks and glared up at her. "No!"

Jason wasn't interested in her office, didn't care about her job, didn't care to meet Caryn. But the photocopy machine was a totally different story. When he saw it in action, he looked up at Sandy, shyly fluttered the lids of his big green eyes and said, "Again? You do that again?" After glancing at Katherine for permission, Sandy shrugged in agreement. From then on out, the trip for Jason became an adventure in color copying.

Satisfied that that much of the excursion was realistic and believable, Katherine led Alex to her office. Caryn automatically looked up from her computer screen, and when she did, Katherine actually thought she saw Caryn's heart stop.

"Oh my God," she said, each word coming out individually, with its own emphasis. "It's you."

Alex smiled. "I hope so. I mean, at least I woke up as myself. I'd hate to be somebody else because I don't know where that person has to go or even what they do for a living."

Katherine looked at Alex as if he were nuts, but Caryn burst into giggles. "Oh, you're so funny!"

"Yes, I am, aren't I?" Alex asked casually, and again Caryn giggled.

Katherine cleared her throat. "I'm going to take Mr. Cane on a tour of the office, Caryn."

Caryn nodded happily.

"Take messages and I'll return calls when Jason and Mr. Cane leave."

Looking joyfully speechless, Caryn nodded again.

"Well, I *think* that went well," Alex observed when they were out of hearing range of Caryn's office.

Katherine breathed a sigh of relief. "It did."

"Ah, do I detect a note in your voice that might mean you're actually beginning to trust me?"

She sighed. "I suppose I am."

"Good. It's about time." He said the last as he was glancing around. His expression became more and more confused, and finally he turned to her. "What, exactly, do you guys do here?"

"Exactly?" she asked, a smile playing on her lips.

"I don't see equipment. I don't see files. I don't see blueprints. I really don't see anything but offices."

"That's because we're here exclusively to help our facilities run at peak efficiency."

"That sounds like PR."

"It is. I wrote it."

"Terrific," Alex said, then looked around again. "So basically you guys don't do anything."

"Sure we do. Not only do we come up with the financing information, the financial backing and keep track of the financial records of each of our landfills, but I actually go out and get the contracts for the trash."

"You buy trash?"

"No, I sell airspace in which we dispose of trash."

She took him to a room in the back, a room that contained the layout plans for each of their facilities. The twelve-color schematics had been framed and hung on the walls of the huge room, which also contained a conference table and chairs.

"Look here," she said, pointing to the design schematic for their largest facility. "The landfill is built in cells. You divide the property into sections and then stack the trash in such a way that eventually you build a mountain."

"It's not like filling in a hole?"

"No, it's building a mountain."

"So, essentially, then, you sell air?" he asked, incredulous.

"Airspace."

"Same difference," he said, then started to laugh.

"What is so funny?" she demanded indignantly.

"You sell air."

"I do not sell air."

"Oh, really? Then what would you call it?"

"Disposal space," she stated succinctly, then haughtily turned away.

"Look, Katherine," he said, moving away from the schematic, and catching her arm as she stalked past him. "I think we've been avoiding the fact that I have plenty of money. You don't *have* to work."

She stared at him. "I thought part of the purpose of your marrying me was to give you a career wife to negate some of your chauvinistic image."

"I never actually set it out that way, but yes, I guess that's part of it. I mean, it certainly wouldn't hurt."

"Well, then, it would be counterproductive for me to quit. Besides, I like my job."

"You *like* selling air?"

"I *like* selling air," she admitted easily. "I like the people I deal with. I like the way my industry—particuarly this company—works hard to keep the environment safe." Along those ends, she turned him toward the engineer's drawing again and explained the synthetic liner and the leachate treatment system, both of which protect the local water supply. She pointed out erosion and sedimentation controls, controls for stemming odors and vectors, and plans for replacing wetlands and reclaiming the mountain once it's built.

Sufficiently amazed, Alex moved away. He cleared his throat. "I never realized how environmentally conscious your industry is."

"Perhaps it's time you started looking at it that way. You know, not everything important is done in a public, grandiose way. Some of the smallest considerations," she said, pointing to a simple net that kept a stream clean by catching runaway trash, "are more important than the big ones." She stopped and smiled at him. "I'd think someone considering a family-oriented television station would be environmentally conscious enough to remember that."

Suddenly, probably because of the way he was staring at her, Katherine got the distinct impression he wasn't paying a whit of attention to anything she'd said. "Fine husband you'll make," she teased lightly. "We're not even married yet and already you're not paying attention to your wife."

He shook his head. "I'm sorry. Did you say something?"

"I said lots of things. You weren't paying one bit of attention."

"That's because I was staring at your dimple." He looked at her. "Do you know you have a dimple?"

"Of course I know I have a dimple."

"Well, Katherine, I think I better tell you it's like one of those little things you were talking about. You know, one of those little things that you hardly think makes any difference but actually it really does."

"What in the hell are you talking about?"

"Your dimple has always been there. But this morning for some reason it's driving me absolutely crazy."

Wide-eyed, she stared at him. "My dimple?"

"Your dimple," he agreed, then astounded her further by placing his hands on her shoulders and bending toward her enough that he could not only softly kiss the slight indentation in her cheek, but place his tongue in it, outlining the shape, examining the contours.

"Stop that," she said, but the words came out as a husky whisper, and if she had a pit to her stomach, it was definitely on the floor.

"No," he simply disagreed, then wrapped his arms around her and pulled her into his embrace. "I like it. I want to keep going," he added before he lowered his head and pressed his lips to hers as if it were the most natural, most logical thing to do. Caught off guard, Katherine found her arms sliding up to his shoulders almost of their own volition. She nearly stopped herself, but the heat of his mouth as he nipped and teased hers completely took all her attention, seizing her memory for other, more important concerns, like meeting his mouth, answering his caresses.

As she thought the last, she pressed her mouth against his, kissing him back as if they'd been longtime lovers. The realization jolted her. Because it was true. The kiss was natural. Genuine. An expression that was every bit as much anticipation as it was hopeful. It was a kiss shared by people experimenting, not playacting. It was a kiss that confirmed that they were beginning to care for each other. A kiss that made her very well aware that one of them had better keep their perspective.

Sighing, she pushed herself out of his arms and away from his tempting mouth. To assure that she wouldn't be enticed to fall into the kiss again, she turned around. When she did, she saw Caryn standing in the doorway, grinning foolishly.

"You two make such a wonderful couple," she said, gushing, a dreamy romanticism dripping through her voice.

"Yes, well..." Katherine said, clearing her throat. "I guess that particular cat's out of the bag."

"We're dating," Alex supplied simply, and both watched Caryn's eyes bug. "Actually, all this started because of Jason, but you know how these things go...."

Caryn nodded appreciatively, and though Alex appeared quite pleased with himself for taking them from the category of people who were trying to share the burden of custody, to two people who were falling in a love as a result of the burden of that custody, Katherine felt strangely betrayed. It was patently clear that he'd walked them into the dimple conversation to change the subject once he spotted Caryn walking down the hall, but even though Katherine knew it was the right thing to do, it still stung.

Worse, though the kiss had been the perfect icing on the cake of the charade, it suddenly felt like an insult. She'd reacted honestly and genuinely to something that for Alex was nothing more than playacting.

Suppressing the urge to drop her head to her hands and groan at her own stupidity, Katherine turned on her heel and walked out of the room. Somewhat bitterly, she realized they'd accomplished everything they set out to do.

The only problem was, it also hurt like hell. Not only because he'd stolen control of the situation and moved it all along according to his own timetable, but for other reasons—reasons that ran so deep, she didn't dare try to dig for their roots.

All she would allow herself to admit was that she hurt.

# *Chapter Six*

"I really wish you would have done this by yourself."

"Oh, come on, Katherine," Alex chided, then straightened the collar of her white blouse before brushing the smooth strands of her auburn hair behind her ears. "You know the only way we're going to convince Judge Black that we're falling in love is if we go to him together, present a united front and all that honest, genuine stuff."

Katherine shook her head in wonder. "That's exactly my point. We are about as far from honest as we can get right now."

"You don't think it's honest and genuine to want to raise our nephew in peace?"

"I think it's the end justifying the means."

"I think it's necessary public relations."

"Call it anything you want, Alex," Katherine said, again shaking her head at the complete absurdity that she would find herself trying to deceive a judge. "But it's lying, and I don't like lying."

"There's a way around that, you know."

Katherine sighed with disgust, ignoring his obvious insinuation and promoting her own rationale instead. "I know. I told you. Let me stay home. You're the one with all the charisma and persuasive charm. You don't need me. You could be convincing without me."

"We are both in a position where we could be convincing as hell. We also wouldn't have to lie," Alex reminded, then grazed his fingertips along the fringe of her collar. A quick, spasmodic quiver ran through Katherine, but she managed to suppress it before it became obvious.

"Stop that," she whispered, but it came out as a shrewish hiss.

"Why? Because you like it?"

"How about because it's embarrassing to have somebody touch me when I'm in public?"

That answer seemed to confuse him, but as he considered it, Katherine could see a realization of some sort dawn on him.

"Is that why you got so mad when I kissed your dimple in front of your secretary?"

"She's not my secretary, she's my administrative assistant."

"I stand corrected. But I'm not going to let you avoid the issue. Did you get angry with me because I kissed you in front of your administrative assistant?"

She considered lying, but knew how hypocritical that would be since their lying was what had started this argument in the first place. "Yes," she said honestly. "I didn't like that you had kissed me in front of her."

"All I did was take advantage of a very tempting situation."

"You threw us into this relationship far too quickly," Katherine said, then stepped away from him, out of the reach of his skilled fingertips.

Alex shrugged. "So what?"

"So that wasn't the deal. You promised me a visit, one visit for my friends and co-workers to get used to you, and you broke your promise."

"I also made a very smooth transition for those very same friends and co-workers, so that our situation would be more believable."

"Yeah, well, it might have worked, but it wasn't what we agreed to."

"Too bad," he said, surprising her when his voice became as hard as granite. "You know, I'm getting damned sick and tired of tiptoeing around your feelings, having to ask for permission for things about Jason, always being the one who takes the blame for everything. Get a grip on reality, here, Katherine. You agreed to this arrangement. Come to think of it, you made the situation public with your boss even before you told me. Did I get mad? Hell, no. Now you start showing me the same kind of consideration, or perhaps I'll check into the possibility of fighting Marissa myself."

His unusual burst of temper shocked her so much, Katherine's eyes widened and she took a quick step backward. "You can't fight Marissa yourself. You've said it a hundred times. Otherwise you wouldn't need me."

"Guess again," he said, then turned away from her. "I sent a private investigator to Montana. He said on the surface everything looks perfectly normal, perfectly wonderful with good old sister Marissa, but there's a rumbling of something in the air, something he hasn't been able to pin down yet. If Marissa's in trouble, or her husband turns out to be a crook, then this case comes down to you and me again." He pivoted and looked at her. All the humor had fled from his crystal-green eyes and in its place was some very stark determination. "And there's no way in hell I'll let you beat me."

Katherine swallowed.

"So maybe, just maybe, this marriage benefits you a lot more than it benefits me. And perhaps a wise woman would stop biting the hand that's only trying to help her."

"Judge Black will see you now."

Startled back to reality, Katherine jumped when Judge Black's secretary entered the reception room and made that announcement. Alex, however, turned casually and gave the fifty-year-old woman his most charming smile. "Why, thank you, Miss Poindexter."

Miss Poindexter returned his smile. "You're welcome, Mr. Cane. Right this way, please."

Alex motioned for Katherine to precede him, and she easily slid past him. But with every step she took, her knees became a little shakier. Not only was she about to lie to a judge, but she realized unless she was convincing this afternoon, Alex would dump her.

She considered that his private investigator's "rumbling" might turn out to be a dead end; however she also remembered Munro telling her about her slim chance of beating Alex in a fight for Jason. She recalled her promise to Jessica, and the sad, yet somehow hopeful, look on Jessica's face when she elicited Katherine's promise to care for Jason.

Without Katherine, Jason would miss something in his life. He wouldn't only miss knowing the other side of his family, he would miss a woman's influence. He would miss learning about gentleness and softness. He would miss learning about kindness and simplicity. Jason needed *her.*

Alex Cane could and probably would give Jason everything a little boy could hope for, but without a woman's touch in the child's life, it wouldn't be worth a tinker's damn.

Given that Alex already admitted he was planning alternative strategies for getting and keeping Jason, and given that her own lawyer had told her her options were practically nil, when Katherine looked into the eyes of Judge Arnold Black, she knew she was looking at her future.

She reached for Alex's hand. He closed his fingers around hers. All in all, it felt very much like selling one's soul to the devil.

"Sit down, please," Judge Black instructed, and Katherine and Alex sat on the black leather seats across from his desk. "I know you're hear to talk with me about Jason, so let's cut to the chase. What has changed in the last four weeks? What piece of information are you bringing me that you believe will change my mind about giving custody to your sister?"

"Well, Your Honor," Alex said, pulling Katherine's hand across their joined armrests, and very close to his heart, "Katherine and I do have something to tell you."

"Does it have anything to do with the way you're holding hands instead of slinging petitions full of accusations?" Judge Black asked craftily.

Alex smiled. "You're very observant."

"No, you're very obvious," the judge countered, sighing heavily. "I suppose now you've come here to tell me that you've fallen in love, you're getting married and you want to keep your nephew."

The sarcastic and insulting tone in the judge's voice made Katherine's heart stop with fear. Clearly he didn't believe them. She felt like an illegal alien trying to pass off a marriage to a taxi driver. But then Alex looked at her—and all those fears disappeared. With one glance, he could make even her believe he actually cared for her.

It was uncanny.

"No, we haven't fallen in love," Alex admitted with a chuckle. "But we do like each other a great deal."

"And you want to keep your nephew."

"Well, we simply don't think it would be fair to ship Jason across the country in the middle of August, only to have us discover at Christmastime that we're going to get married."

"And what if you discover you hate each other at Christmastime?"

Alex shrugged. "Then Jason's enjoyed our company for another year. One year," Alex emphasized. "That's all we're asking. One year to see if this relationship has any merit."

Sighing, the judge leaned back in his old, creaking chair. "Why?" he asked simply. Then, as if suddenly furious, he slapped his hands on his desk. "Why should I do this?"

"Because we're Jason's closest living relatives," Katherine reminded him cautiously. "Because I promised my sister I would raise her son," she added, looking directly into the old man's eyes. "And because Alex and I truly do like and respect each other," she said, and found that she actually hadn't lied. She did sort of like Alex. He was pleasant to have around, and he was successful enough to respect. That rationalization bolstered her confidence, and she held the judge's gaze again. "That's actually a better basis for a marital relationship than most people have."

"Are you trying to tell me that you like each other as friends, but don't find each other attractive?"

Alex burst into unrestrained laughter. "I certainly didn't say that."

The judge looked at Katherine. "Katherine?"

"Yes?" Katherine asked, not quite sure what the judge wanted her to say.

"Do you or do you not find Mr. Cane attractive?"

"That's kind of a personal question, sir."

"This is kind of a personal custody battle. I want your nephew to live in a stable, comfortable, wonderful home. You and Mr. Cane want to keep him. Four weeks ago, you came into my courtroom hating each other. Now you tell me you like each other, that you think you may actually consider a marital relationship. I personally find it extremely hard to swallow. And frankly I'm very annoyed that you'd bring this kind of insanity to me. That you'd waste my time this way—"

"Now wait a minute," Alex interrupted, but the judge turned on him like an old, mean bulldog.

"No, *you* wait a minute. I had my staff do a little more digging on you, since I knew that if anybody would appeal, it would be you," he said, his gaze holding Alex's.

"And?" Alex asked quietly.

"And I know that you're not really Jason's uncle."

Katherine's mouth dropped open in surprise, but Alex didn't even bat an eyelash. "That's not exactly true. Ryan and I were half brothers, so technically I am still Jason's uncle."

"Half uncle," the judge reminded him angrily. "I resent that you hid that information from me...."

"I didn't hide that information from you."

"If you don't consider not putting a pertinent fact into a petition for custody, then you're splitting hairs."

The argument ebbed and flowed around Katherine the same way water bounced around a buoy. Sometimes she could stay on top of it. Other times she felt it pull her under. Since Marissa was only Alex's half sister, it explained why they weren't close, why they didn't pretend to want to be close. However, Alex's watered-down blood ties to Jason explained why Alex had been so eager, so agreeable to finding an alternative to fighting Marissa for custody.

Despite the fact that Alex had hidden this information from her, too, and really was as sneaky as Jessica always contended, one simple truth remained. For a woman who so desperately sought to raise her brother's son, Marissa Peligrini was conspicuously absent from Jason's life. As Alex so skillfully pointed out, Marissa might have filed a petition for custody, but she'd never once even tried to contact Jason.

Unfortunately, that didn't seem to be a consideration with the judge at all.

But Alex's level of commitment was obvious. Not only had he pushed himself into Jason's life, he'd come up with the plan to keep himself in Jason's life.

But that didn't seem to faze the judge, either.

"I am not a stupid old man—"

"Yes, you are," Katherine contradicted suddenly, jumping from her seat. Her heart was beating a hundred times a second, because she'd never done anything like this in her entire life. But she was so tired of fighting and so tired of the way the judge couldn't seem to see the obvious, that she couldn't stop herself. She'd hit her breaking point. She'd tried being reasonable, tried behaving within the confines of the law, but now she was fighting her last battle for Jessica's son. She could feel it in her bones. The mere fact that the judge had further investigated Alex Cane proved that in his mind the decision had already been made. And she'd lost. Actually, Katherine hadn't even gotten enough attention or consideration to warrant an investigation. It was as if she weren't even a part of this custody battle at all.

"I love Jason, I love Jason with my whole heart and soul. I took care of him during his mother's entire illness," she added, bracing her hands on the judge's desk and leaning forward so that she could look him square in the eye. "But you don't give a damn, do you? You just plain don't give a damn. You found a pat, easy answer—a married couple with kids and a ranch. Utopia. And you're going to send my nephew away. Away from me, despite the fact that I loved and cared for him when he really needed somebody to love and care for him."

With all that said, she spun around and ran toward the door. Tears were brimming in her eyes because she was tired of pretending everything was okay. She was even tired of pretending she didn't quite like Alex Cane. She did like him. She liked him a lot. She almost didn't care that he hadn't mentioned he was only a half brother because it was obvious he'd thought it a necessary omission or he wouldn't get Jason. It seemed to her he had more common sense about Jason's welfare than the judge who was charged with the responsibility of finding a good home for their nephew.

"Come on, sweetheart," she said. "I think we're wasting our time with this man."

She stormed out of the room, not caring that she'd probably blown their chances and not even realizing that Alex wasn't following her. It wasn't until she was on the courthouse steps that she saw she was alone, but pride would not allow her to bound back into the judge's chambers and get Alex. She was mad. Furious. How could that rotten old man take her nephew away and give him to people no one knew? Why didn't *she* have the money to investigate? Why didn't Alex tell her *he* was investigating? And why wasn't his investigator working faster? What were their options? How could this happen? How could this judge, a man who didn't even know her, Jason or Alex, make the most important decision of their lives?

Katherine paced the courthouse steps while she mentally ranted. She was still deep in furious thought when Alex ran up behind her.

"He's giving us our year."

Katherine turned round brown eyes on him. "He is?"

"He is," Alex said and laughed heartily. "If I didn't know how much you hated to be kissed in public, I'd kiss you right now." He gave her a look as if waiting for consent. When it wasn't forthcoming, he lifted her off her feet and spun her around. "And do you know why he changed his mind?"

Dazed from the spin and the unexpected news, Katherine shook her head.

"Because you called me sweetheart."

That brought her mental state to peak capacity. *How in the...why in the...had she done that?* "Slip of the tongue. I was thinking about Jason."

"It doesn't matter," Alex said. Then as if he couldn't help himself, he grabbed her again and hugged her. "The judge is really skeptical about us. He's almost positive this is a ploy. But he does see the merit in our argument and rather than rule immediately on Jason's custody, he's going to grant you temporary custody for the next year."

Katherine swallowed. Even as he jubilantly gave her this news, Katherine considered that with temporary custody for the next year, she could keep Jason all to herself. She didn't need Alex anymore.

Then she remembered her job and she bit her lip. She did need him.

And more important, Jason needed him.

With a deep breath, she looked up at the man who, like it or not, was in her life. She remembered that he was tired

# PLAY
## SILHOUETTE'S
# LUCKY HEARTS GAME

## AND YOU GET

- ★ FREE BOOKS
- ★ A FREE GIFT
- ★ AND MUCH MORE

**TURN THE PAGE AND DEAL YOURSELF IN**

# PLAY "LUCKY HEARTS" AND GET . . .

★ **Exciting Silhouette Romance™ novels — FREE**

★ **PLUS a lovely Pearl Drop Necklace — FREE**

# THEN CONTINUE YOUR LUCKY STREAK WITH A SWEETHEART OF A DEAL

1. Play Lucky Hearts as instructed on the opposite page.
2. Send back this card and you'll receive brand-new Silhouette Romance™ novels. These books have a cover price of $2.99 each, but they are yours to keep absolutely free.
3. There's no catch. You're under no obligation to buy anything. We charge nothing — ZERO — for your first shipment. And you don't have to make any minimum number of purchases — not even one!
4. The fact is thousands of readers enjoy receiving books by mail from the Silhouette Reader Service. They like the convenience of home delivery...they like getting the best new novels months before they're available in stores...and they love our discount prices!
5. We hope that after receiving your free books you'll want to remain a subscriber. But the choice is yours — to continue or cancel, anytime at all! So why not take us up on our invitation, with no risk of any kind. You'll be glad you did!

## THE SILHOUETTE READER SERVICE™: HERE'S HOW IT WORKS

Accepting free books places you under no obligation to buy anything. You may keep the books and gift and return the shipping statement marked "cancel". If you do not cancel, about a month later we'll send you 6 additional novels, and bill you just $2.44 each plus 25¢ delivery and applicable sales tax, if any.* That's the complete price—and compared to cover prices of $2.99 each—quite a bargain! You may cancel at anytime, but if you choose to continue, every month we'll send you 6 more books, which you may either purchase at the discount price...or return at our expense and cancel your subscription.

*Terms and prices subject to change without notice. Sales tax applicable in N.Y.

If offer card is missing, write to: Silhouette Reader Service, 3010 Walden Ave, PO Box 1867, Buffalo, NY 14269-1867

NO POSTAGE
NECESSARY
IF MAILED
IN THE
UNITED STATES

**BUSINESS REPLY MAIL**

FIRST CLASS MAIL PERMIT NO. 717 BUFFALO, NY

POSTAGE WILL BE PAID BY ADDRESSEE

SILHOUETTE READER SERVICE
3010 WALDEN AVE
PO BOX 1867
BUFFALO NY 14240-9952

of her whining and complaining. She remembered that he wanted some respect and appreciation. She decided he was right on all counts. "Thank you very much."

"You did it," Alex reminded, draping his arm across her shoulders. "You called me sweetheart," he said, smiling so broadly the expression rivaled the sun.

"Just don't get too cozy with that," Katherine said, but even as the words slipped between her lips, she knew he could get as cozy as he wished because even with a temporary custody order from a judge, she wasn't a good enough guardian. Like it or not, she needed Alex Cane desperately. Maybe even more desperately than he needed her. After all, even as nothing more than a half uncle, he'd gotten more consideration than Katherine—despite the fact that she was a full aunt, temporary guardian and the person into whose care Jessica had delivered her son.

It was an incredibly humbling realization.

## *Chapter Seven*

"I think you should choose a bedroom and start bringing your clothes here."

Katherine glanced up at Alex. He sat at his desk, supposedly reading some proposed legislation that would directly affect his cable networks. Instead, it appeared his mind had been elsewhere.

"Excuse me?" she asked, confused.

Jason and Ronald were collecting autumn leaves, while she and Alex were spending time together in the library. Though a normal couple probably wouldn't have used their evenings reading contracts or legislation, for two workaholics like Alex and Katherine, an evening in the library was more believable than moonlight strolls. Both strove to act as they would if Alex and Katherine really were about to get married—with a few notable exceptions—and both agreed that meant staying close to reality. And they stayed so close to reality that the situation and the routine actually became relatively relaxed. In fact, the announcement of their engagement was only a week away.

"I said, I think you should start moving in."

She shook her head. "Not until my parents are more comfortable."

"Your parents are coming around."

"Maybe, but don't forget they haven't actually seen us together. They've only spoken with us... and only on the phone... and only about Jason."

"Then maybe we should have an engagement party."

She blinked. "Just like that?"

"Just like that," he agreed, and snapped his fingers as if by magic he could make the whole thing appear.

A month ago, Katherine wouldn't have expected Alex to suggest spending time with her parents; two weeks ago it might have been iffy; but tonight, it wasn't all that odd. Alex had already made two phone calls to her dad and he'd even spoken with her mother on the pretense of telling a funny story about Jason. He'd finally realized that their whole reason for getting married—Jason—was also a common denominator, a common ground, with her parents, and he was smoothing out rough spots quickly.

Still, Katherine thought an engagement party might be stretching things. "My parents can't afford to fly to Pennsylvania at the drop of a hat," she said, then returned to her reading.

"I'll send a plane for them."

Sighing, she looked up from the contract and gave him her full attention. Even though they were in a contrived situation, she'd learned a great deal about Alex Cane in the past several weeks, and one of those things was that when he got a bee in his bonnet, he didn't let it go. The other thing was, he didn't bring up subjects or ideas arbitrarily. He'd been planning this.

"All right," she said, sighing again as she set her contract on the leather sofa. "Out with it."

"Well, I think an engagement party would make the wedding happen more easily. I mean, we're getting married the last week of November, because your parents would be here for Thanksgiving anyway, but I've been thinking that with the holiday being the first opportunity for your parents to see you and Jason since Jessica's death, the whole situation's going to turn into more of a sad time than a happy event."

She'd worried about that, too, but she didn't think there was any help for it. She kept forgetting that this man had enough money to solve problems like purchasing plane tickets. And, in all truth, when she did remember it, she didn't feel comfortable imposing.

She probably never would.

"Who would we invite, besides my parents?" she asked quietly.

He smiled, obviously seeing she was coming around, if not already agreeing. On one hand, it pleased her to help do her part to make things run smoothly between them. On the other hand, it disturbed her to be so happy every time she saw he was pleased. They were building bonds and bridges with leaps and bounds, and as necessary as that was, it was happening with an alarming speed and ease. Almost as if they really did love each other.

Which they didn't, she assured herself for the one thousandth time that day.

"As far as I'm concerned, I'd prefer not to invite Marissa."

Katherine chuckled. "You won't get an argument out of me on that one."

"Otherwise, aside from some close friends and a few business associates, I have one cousin. I'd really like for her to be with us for both the engagement party and the wedding. Unfortunately, half the time I don't know where she is, but for this I'll find her."

He said it with such sincerity, Katherine shifted on her seat. He was enjoying this, making the most of it. And though that was endearing, it was also disturbing. Before this was all over with, she was going to hurt him or he was going to hurt her. She could feel it as clearly as the way the air crackled with lightning before a big storm.

"And I think we should invite everybody from your office."

She nodded. "Yes, that would be great," she admitted noncommittally.

"And I think there's something bothering you."

"There's nothing bothering me," she said quickly, looking over at him and smiling. She wasn't going to burst his bubble. He'd been too good to her, too good to Jason and incredibly considerate of her parents, for her to tell him to cool his heels and remember they weren't really getting married, only pretending. She would go along with this if it killed her and, on some level of her persona, it probably would.

Removing his glasses, he rose from his seat and walked to the sofa on which she sat. "I'm sorry," he said soothingly as he sat beside her. His arm went across the back of the couch, and therefore around her shoulders as easily as if it belonged there. "You're very busy, and I'm very demanding."

"You're not very demanding," she conceded shyly, embarrassed that she'd put him into yet another uncomfortable spot.

He reached over and took her chin in such a way that he could force her to look at him. "Would you tell me if I was?"

She laughed. "Yes."

Nodding his agreement, he smiled. "Make sure that you do because I don't want to put you into any situations that are difficult for you to deal with."

"Actually, the whole thing has been surprisingly easy."

"Yes, it has."

"I mean, everything has fallen into place so well..."

"Almost as if we're made for each other," Alex finished for her when she couldn't seem to form the words herself. Side by side, his one arm resting around her shoulders, his hand tilting her face upward, putting his mouth only a whisper away from hers, Katherine felt an ease and contentment beyond description. A few short months ago, she didn't even know this man. Now she not only knew him, she liked him.

A part of her, a part she refused to acknowledge but which fought its way out during situations like this one, wished she were marrying him for all the right reasons.

She sometimes sensed he wished it, too.

Feeling a thrumming of her heart that was almost painful, Katherine extricated herself from his hold. "I've got to go," she whispered, then rose from her seat. "I'll find Jason, and Ronald can let us out."

"Katherine, you can't run from this forever."

"And you can't have it both ways," she countered, facing him, not even bothering to pretend she didn't understand what he was talking about. "The only way we can get married for real is if we step out of this commitment to Jason and date for real."

He leaned back on the couch. "From the tone of your voice I can tell you're not willing to take that risk."

She drew a long, shaky breath. "No, I'm not. I believe there's a magic in this moment that's making us feel things we don't really feel. I think that if we took this relationship into the real world, we'd hate each other. And we also would have thrown away the opportunity to reach goals we can't afford to miss. I'd either lose my job or lose Jason. And no matter how much you think you're going to find a chink in your sister's armor, you haven't found one in two months. You're only a half uncle, not a full aunt like Marissa. Without this marriage, you'd lose Jason, too."

"Aren't you being a little melodramatic?"

"Face it, Alex. If we dated for real and it didn't work out, the judge would have us back in court before the end of the year. And this time we'd be angry, emotional. And Marissa really would end up with Jason."

"You're wrong," he said quietly, though he had to admit she did have some valid points. The one he refused to think about or acknowledge was the fact that there was magic in the moment that was leading them to feel things they didn't feel. He liked her, he really liked her, and he would hate to think that the first time in his life that he dropped his guard and let someone in, it was only because he was protected by their commitment to Jason. He wanted to believe there was something special about her, not safety in their commitment, that made this time together so wonderful, so peacefully, blissfully perfect.

She shook her head. "And you're a dreamer." With that she turned and walked out of the library.

In fact, she didn't set foot in Alex's home again until the night before the engagement party, when she took Alex's advice and brought bits and pieces of her wardrobe.

With the cool precision of someone seeking only to fulfill a goal, she walked through the six possible bedroom choices and in the end decided she couldn't yet decide. Ronald stored her clothing in the large closet of the room located in the center of all six rooms, and then she took Jason home as if there was nothing special, nothing unusual going to happen the following day. Even though she was about to face her moment of truth—convincing her parents she was happily marrying a man who was wrong for her. Completely wrong. If he couldn't get along with Jessica, who was sweet and kind and a hundred times more wonderful than Katherine could ever be, then how could Katherine possibly think he was a man worth loving? And what would Jessica have thought of Katherine's plans to not only marry Alex, but to allow her bitter enemy to raise her son? Why hadn't she thought of this sooner? How could she do this? How could she betray Jessica this way? Wasn't this sort of betraying her parents? What if they saw right through this and exposed her...publicly? In front of her boss, her friends, her co-workers . . . the judge!

Katherine and Alex planned to meet her parents at the airport at eleven, but first Katherine went to work. Her nerves had to be calmed before she greeted her parents—fiancé and child on her arm—and she thought spending some time in the office, getting her mind off the situation, might break the awful horror of impending doom that seemed to be surrounding her.

It didn't.

At nine-thirty, Caryn strode into her office, slammed the door and plopped herself on the chair across from Katherine's desk. "What in the hell is the matter with you?" she demanded angrily. "It's the day of your engagement party and not only are you at work instead of at home gaily arranging centerpieces, you're as grouchy as a bear with a thorn in its paw!"

Unexpectedly and as suddenly as a spring shower, Katherine burst into tears.

Caryn bounded around the desk to pat Katherine's shoulder sympathetically. "All right. I'm getting the picture here. You're nervous."

"Oh, Caryn," Katherine said, gathering her wits because she didn't quite understand why she was crying. "You don't understand!"

"Of course I do," Caryn said soothingly. "You're marrying a very rich, very important man."

"I could handle that," Katherine disagreed, then rose from her seat and began to pace.

"Really?" Caryn asked as she settled herself against Katherine's credenza. "I don't think I could. But if you can and that's not what's bothering you, then what's the problem?"

Katherine groped in her mind for a logical explanation and, finding none, she sighed heavily. "Don't you think all this is a little convenient?" she asked quietly.

"What?"

"That Alex and I both want Jason, that marrying him solves problems for me and gives him the politically correct wife he needs to dispel his horrible reputation?"

Caryn tilted her head. "Honestly? Yes. But you've always admitted that those are the things that brought you together."

"And they'll keep us together."

"But?" Caryn pressed because of the doubt that dripped through Katherine's words.

"But he doesn't love me," Katherine whispered honestly.

"Oh, Katherine," Caryn said, jumping to Katherine's side again. "How can you say that?"

"Because he's a man of the world, accustomed to smarter, sexier, more sophisticated women than me—" she admitted, voicing feelings she didn't even know she had. When she realized what she was doing, what she was admitting, she paused, and took a shuddering breath. Knowing she couldn't stop what she'd started, Katherine made her final, most honest admission. "Caryn, don't you see? This marriage benefits him enough that he could merely *think* he's fallen in love—"

"Oh, you're such a skeptic," Caryn interrupted, patting Katherine's shoulder. "Even though I agree that you have the right to some last-minute jitters, that doesn't mean I agree with your rationale. Discounting love, honor, trust and respect, I think Alex gains far less in this marriage than you seem to feel he does. I think Alex loves you. And you ought to start trusting him."

"Yeah, well, don't get too comfortable with this," she warned Caryn, though inside she knew she was really warning herself. "Because to me it's all very fragile."

"Most love is," Caryn agreed, then turned Katherine toward the door of her office. "Go to the lady's room, fix your face, blow your nose and then scram. We'll hold the fort for the rest of the day. And see you tonight."

Katherine forced a smile, and realized she did feel much, much better. "You're a good friend."

"And you're just a nervous bride-to-be," Caryn said, smiling at her friend. "I'll be behind you every step of the way. I'm right here if you need to talk again. I'm not going to let you let this one get away."

Katherine chuckled softly, comforted by the fact that even if she was going into a pretend marriage, she still had one very good friend.

By the time she arrived at Alex's house to board the limo, she did feel much, much better. It had been difficult holding in all her conflicting feelings, and even though Caryn was basing her opinions on some misinformation, somehow her encouragement hit its mark.

With her emotions tucked away in a secure corner, Katherine held a civil, interesting conversation with Alex.

She even let him squeeze her fingers reassuringly, as they stood in the small terminal of Johnstown's airport.

Katherine's mother stepped into the one-room terminal.

"Jason!" Mary Whitman cried. Dropping her carry-on bag, she ran to Alex and pulled Jason from his arms. "Oh, Jason! It's so wonderful to see you."

Jason's face scrunched up in confusion and Katherine could see that any second he would burst into tears.

"Take him," Alex whispered in Katherine's ear, as he nudged her forward, toward her mother.

She shook her head. "No, we're a team now," she reminded him, then turned and smiled at him. "Equals. You get him."

Returning her smile, Alex lifted Jason from Mary Whitman's arms as her father approached. "Here, Mrs. Whitman, let me take him. Any second now he's going to be screaming."

"Mr. Cane," Katherine's father said, inclining his head.

After shifting Jason to his other arm, Alex extended his hand. "Please, call me Alex," he instructed, shaking Katherine's father's hand.

"Alex," Richard Whitman said. "You, of course, know my wife, Mary."

Alex nodded and said, "Hello."

"Well, then," Katherine said, sighing with something that felt very much like relief, "let's get going."

"Aren't you going to hug your father?" Richard asked solemnly.

"Oh, of course, Dad," Katherine said, surprised that she'd made such a stupid mistake. "I'm sorry," she added as she pulled his bulky body against her. Her short, round father grunted his approval, then pulled away. Without another thought, she hugged her mother who, with her auburn hair and slim build, was the spitting image of what Katherine knew she would look like twenty years from now.

"It's so good to see you," Mary said, and Katherine could hear the tears in her voice.

"Well, you're going to be seeing a lot of me for the next few days. I took some time off."

Pleased, Alex faced her. "You did?"

She drew a long breath. "Caryn thinks I've been working too hard."

"Wise woman," Alex agreed, then put his arm around her shoulders and pulled her close enough that he could kiss her forehead. The gesture was so appealing, simply romantic and sincere that even Katherine felt a strange relief from it. Her parents, she noticed, visibly relaxed.

They spent the afternoon touring the estate grounds, getting settled into their rooms and in general spending time with Jason. Katherine caught her mother crying twice, and her father crying once, and knew beyond a shadow of a doubt that Alex had been correct. This engagement party really would take the edge off their wedding.

To save time, she'd decided to dress for the party at Alex's house but, despite the fact that her parents had settled in reasonably well, she was so nervous, she couldn't seem to get herself moving. Eventually, she decided on a simple blue sequined gown. Fitted to the contours of her body, it fell in one long line. Its only hint at cleverness was one bared shoulder. She pulled her hair to the top of her head and let it fall in a bundle of curls that didn't quite reach the nape of her neck. Rhinestone earrings sparkled on her lobes, but otherwise she decided against jewelry. She felt exposed tonight, vulnerable. But somehow, adding jewelry would have seemed too much of a pretense.

Satisfied that she looked as good as she could under the circumstances, Katherine left the bedroom and began to glide down the spiral staircase. The light from the enormous crystal chandelier of the foyer bounced off the sequins of her dress, and even to Katherine the effect seemed dramatic. With every step she took down the staircase, she felt stronger, more beautiful. When she glanced at the bottom to find Alex staring up at her, a look of undisguised appreciation on his incredibly handsome face, she began to understand why.

He was becoming her strength. Oddly enough, she was letting him.

"You are beautiful," he whispered as he reached up to take her fingers and lead her down the remaining four steps.

"Thank you," she accepted graciously. "I'm sorry if I missed greeting your guests."

"Don't apologize," he said, then kissed her fingers. "You were worth the wait."

Tucking her fingers around his elbow, he led her into the living room. Standing among the bundles of flowers, the guests looked like part of a large, elaborate bouquet. Alex introduced her to some business associates she'd yet to meet and reacquainted her with others. Munro preened, Ralph Fasulo scowled, but the judge seemed to find Ralph's open disapproval as a sort of stamp of approval that the engagement was genuine. All in all, everything went tremendously well. Even her parents found entertainment and good company with two couples who were older business associates of Alex.

They retired to the dining room and ate a feast fit for kings, then Katherine turned to Alex and suggested that it might be time for them to put Jason to bed. Or at least put him out of his misery by letting him go to his room with Ronald.

Alex put his elbow on the table and his chin on the palm of his hand while she spoke. He watched her face as she talked and listened to her in such a way that she felt like a trusted confidante; then he smiled and nodded his head once. "I think you're right, but I have one announcement to make first."

Katherine felt her stomach fall to the floor. The word *announcement* made her nervous. She glanced at the door, saw it was open and waiting, but she stayed put anyway. This was the right thing to do. Jason was happy. Alex was happy. Her parents approved. His friends and business associates beamed with joy. Her friends and business associates thought she was the luckiest woman in the world. Backing out now would be the act of a coward. She stayed right where she was.

Alex rose.

"Ladies and gentlemen," he said, glancing at the fifty or so guests who lined the long, elaborate dining table. "We all know why we're here."

The guests broke into a comfortable patter of whispers and Katherine glanced at Caryn just in time to get a thumbs-up signal from her joyous administrative assistant.

"But there is one little detail that I think most of you are waiting for."

Confused, Katherine looked up at him. He took her hand and when she thought he would urge her to rise, he surprised her by dropping to one knee beside her chair.

"Katherine," he said, then took a long breath that sounded unexpectedly shaky. Even as he said her name, Ronald appeared at his side, a satin pillow in his white-gloved hands. Alex turned slightly and plucked a sparkling item from the pillow, then faced her again. "Will you do me the honor of becoming my wife?" he asked softly, his face a study in hopefulness as he held the ring poised at the third finger of her left hand.

She swallowed. The ring was comprised of a single solitaire, which had to be at least two carats. Flanking the glittering diamond were two heart-shaped diamonds, each of which looked to be a carat.

"I designed it myself," he said, again whispering, again sounding like an unsure suitor.

The ring winked at her. Katherine blinked back tears.

"You don't like it?" he asked quietly.

"My God, it's the most beautiful thing I've ever seen," she answered honestly, her voice choked with tears.

"Then say you'll marry me."

"Just to get a ring?" she asked stupidly, but somehow it felt like a logical question.

"I was sort of hoping you were marrying me for other things, but if the ring sways your opinion, please take it into consideration."

It was only because their guests laughed that Katherine remembered there were other people in the room. She remembered that the ring was for their benefit. She remembered her promises and her commitments.

She glanced at Alex, her heart beating in her throat.

"Yes," she said simply. "I'll marry you."

He slipped the ring on her finger and Katherine felt the weight of every stone.

Then the heartache that she knew would follow.

## *Chapter Eight*

Katherine drew in a long breath. The knot in her stomach seemed to grow with every minute that passed. For the life of her she couldn't remember why she was doing this. Her mind was a total blank.

"Oh, Katherine," Caryn gushed, coming up behind Katherine who stood before the full-length mirror of what was now officially her bedroom in Alex Cane's home. "You're the most beautiful bride I've ever seen."

She tried not to be. It wasn't that she wanted to make it obvious that there was something amiss in these proceedings. It wasn't that she wasn't excited about dressing up. The problem was, she *was* excited about dressing up. This wedding had excited her a little too much.

So she'd tried to downplay the situation. Though she wore pearls, her dress was simple. The scoop-neck was edged in satin piping, but the long white gown wasn't covered with beads or sequins or even lace. Instead, it depended upon the simple beauty of heavy white velvet for its attractiveness. There was no full, belled skirt, no unusual shape to the design. It was an unpretentious, form-fitting gown with folds of material gathered at the small of her back and held in place by a large satin bow.

Her shoulder-length auburn hair had been swept up into a neat roll and tucked beneath a sophisticated hat. Little tendrils kissed her neck. A small veil gave her the look of a woman of mystery. Her crimson lipstick accented her alabaster skin, but instead of looking sickly, she somehow seemed to look innocent. Mysterious and innocent. Katherine felt as though she might as well be wearing a sign that announced something wasn't quite right with this wedding.

For all her attempts to look good, but not too good, happy, but not falsely so, involved in, but not overwhelmed by, the proceedings, she failed miserably. The gorgeous dress made her look elegant. The twinkle in her eyes gave away her true feelings. And the knot in her stomach was her own private testimonial that these proceedings meant more to her, much, much more to her, than she wanted them to.

"Katherine?"

Both Katherine and Caryn turned at the sound of her father's call. She cleared her throat. "We're ready, Dad. You can come in."

"Thank God," he said, chuckling as he stepped through her bedroom door. "They seated your mother ten minutes ago. The crowd is getting restless."

Laughing airily, Katherine ducked her head away from her father. He wasn't a particularly observant man. He was a happy man. A joking, happy, funny guy. But she was shaking like a leaf in a hurricane, and he didn't have to be clairvoyant, or even slightly sensitive, to notice something was wrong.

"Uh, Caryn?" Richard Whitman said, turning to face Katherine's friend. "Could you give us a minute alone?"

"Sure," she happily said, turning to walk out of the room. Her flowing green satin gown swished and danced as she made her way to the door.

When she was gone, Katherine's father took both of her hands. "Kate," he said, and the knot in her stomach tightened. "You're shaking, and your hands are like ice."

She smiled. "I know."

"I've heard of brides getting cold feet, but you've got one hell of a case of cold hands here."

"Do you suppose that means the same thing as cold feet? That I'm about to bolt?" she teased, trying to lighten the mood.

"Thinking about it?" he inquired, his eyebrows arching.

She shook her head. "No, no," she assured with false brightness that actually sounded very real.

"Good," Richard said, then he sighed. "You know, Kate, I'm not skillful at these sentimental things. But I have to tell you this has got to be the happiest day of my life. We were a little skeptical about Alex, because Jessica—" He stopped, his Adam's apple bobbing as the thoughts of his daughter caught him off guard. After swallowing, he continued. "Jessica and Alex had their problems."

She squeezed his fingers. "Hey, I know, Dad. I know there were lots of problems. But things are different between Alex and me. Things are different with Alex," she said, then realized she wasn't lying. It was true. Alex was different, very, very different from the man he'd been even four months ago when they'd decided to marry.

Suddenly more confused than ever, she squeezed her father's hands again. "Come on, big guy. If we don't get moving, there'll be an angry mob marching up here to get us."

"You're right," Richard agreed, chuckling. "Let's go, Katie. You're about to marry money."

His statement made her laugh and she was grateful, but by the time they walked down the long hall and made their appearance at the top of the spiral staircase, the laughter was gone again. Her knees felt like rubber, her breaths shivered in her chest and tears—real, honest-to-God tears—were gathering in her eyes.

She didn't want to do this.

Because she *did* want to do this.

She really, honestly wanted to be marrying this man.

My God! She loved him.

Tears shimmered on the edge of her eyelid as she walked down the steps, through the foyer and to the entrance of the large living room. Immediately, all eyes turned in her direction, the string quartet began to play, but Katherine froze. At the head of the room, in front of the minister, beside a beaming, obviously ecstatic Denny, who filled in at the last minute because neither of Alex's cousins could make the wedding, stood Alex Cane, holding Jason perched on the crook of his arm.

Neither black tuxedo had been rented. Both had been made specifically for Katherine's two men. Jason looked as cute and cuddly as a koala bear. But Alex looked elegant, wonderful, as worldly and sophisticated as he was. Yet somehow charmingly appealing with his little counterpart on his arm. Alex's simple boyish haircut enhanced his refined good looks. His eyes were as bright and beautiful as the beam of late-fall sunlight in which he was ensconced. Not only was he the most attractive man she knew, the best kisser in the world, the most seductively appealing tempter of virtue, but he owned everything in this room, everything in this house, everything for a full mile radius. He loved people, cared about causes, wanted to change the world...

And she was marrying him.

They reached Alex quickly, and he turned and handed Jason to Denny. As her father released her hand, placing it into Alex's open palm, Katherine felt an odd sensation, like a shifting. It was almost as if she actually felt her life changing. She felt the sudden loss of everything she was leaving behind. She felt a surge of excitement and fear over everything she was stepping into. A physical commotion filled her chest. All of this was supposed to be a game. If not a game, a proposition, an arrangement of convenience...

So why did it feel so real? Why was she losing things she didn't want to lose and gaining things she didn't want to gain?

Alex's fingers closed around hers. As his warmth enveloped her cold, cold hand, some part of him seemed to seep into her. Her heart began hammering against her chest. They were supposed to turn and face the minister, and though she'd expected Alex to guide her into doing that, he stood still, immobile. It took a second before she caught on that he was waiting for her to look up at him. Slowly she raised her gaze from their joined hands to the face of the man she only seconds ago realized she loved, and when she did, the expression in his eyes stopped her heart.

The beauty of the bright emerald color of his eyes went unnoticed as she absorbed the look of near adoration he poured over her. He couldn't tell her she looked beautiful, so he said it with a look, and he said it well... poetically. Then he brought her fingers to his lips and with a brush so light and reverent, as soft as the touch of a feather, he kissed her fingers, held them to his lips for a few meaningful seconds, then turned her to face the minister.

Katherine fought to quell her tears. They wanted to burst out. She wanted to turn and run. She wanted to stay and make the commitment. She wanted to face the crowd and tell them the truth. She wanted to take him aside and confess that she loved him and ask him—no, beg him—to feel the same way about her.

In the end, she did nothing so dramatic. She made her vows to Alex Cane exactly as she'd promised. And she knew in her heart she had every intention of keeping them, and in keeping them she would experience the greatest pain she's ever known because he didn't love her. To him this marriage was merely a business deal.

That dash of reality calmed her enough that the walk back down the aisle was actually uneventful. She smiled and nodded to the misty-eyed guests and didn't even feel a qualm of conscience. They'd done this for good reasons. Excellent reasons. Alex had the money and power, and the plans for his new television station were revolutionary enough to change the world. The entertainment world needed someone levelheaded and strong like Alex. Just as Jason needed someone as levelheaded and strong as Alex. But Jason also needed her and she'd made a promise to Jessica, which she had every intention of keeping.

They greeted guests with smiles and hugs and a few sloppy-cheeked kisses. Eventually, the receiving line grew small enough that Ronald began directing everyone into the dining room. Katherine automatically turned to follow suit, but Alex caught her hand.

"Wait a second," he said, giving her a warm, loving smile that caused her heart to do a little flip-flop. Everyone seemed to have disappeared as if by magic and she and

Alex were alone for the first time in days. "I have something for you."

She swallowed. "You do? Oh, Alex, I'm sorry, I never thought to... I mean, I..."

He started to laugh. "Will you relax? It's okay."

"Okay, but I hope you're not going to make a habit of this."

"Actually, I am," he said, reaching into the breast pocket of his tuxedo jacket. "I've never had so much fun choosing a gift for a woman. You're the most exciting person I've ever bought for."

She smiled. "Why? Because I have nothing so you can buy me absolutely anything and know I'll need it?"

"That's part of it," he admitted, grinning. "The other part is you're very beautiful and anything in that jewelry store would look absolutely stunning on you."

His words caused her heart to do one of those flip-flops again, but this time her chest also tightened painfully. "Alex, maybe it's not such a good idea for me to get used to you buying me gifts."

"Nonsense. You're my wife. This is part of my pleasure."

She expected him to say, you're my wife, you must be seen wearing beautiful things, so when he said what he did, her eyes snapped upward. His smiling expression squeezed her heart even harder.

"Here," he said, handing her the small jeweler's box. "Thank you for marrying me."

Tears filled her eyes again, and she pressed her lips together as she accepted the box. It felt so right, so good, so real, she almost couldn't handle it.

"Open it."

She did as he asked, her shaking fingers making a mess out of the neat silver foil. When the paper was off the box, he took it from her, freeing her hands to spring the box lid.

Nestled into folds of velvet were pearl earrings, but they were trimmed with small, elegant, winking diamonds.

"They're beautiful," she whispered, looking up at him again.

"So are you," he said and bent slightly to place a soft, chaste kiss on her lips. He pulled away and simply stared at her for a second, searching her eyes. Katherine's heart began to hammer in her chest. She felt a pull, the magnetism they shared urging her forward. This time when their lips met, their kiss was neither chaste nor soft. Almost six months of pent-up frustration and passion seemed to come pouring out of nowhere as their mouths met, open and hungry. Their tongues twined almost of their own volition, and Katherine stepped forward into his waiting arms.

She didn't know how long they stood that way; she only knew that the sound that interrupted them was loud enough that the maker had done it intentionally. They jumped apart guiltily, but as if he realized they'd gotten married and didn't have anything to be guilty about, Alex caught her hand and pulled her close to him again.

"I'm sorry, Mr. Cane," Ronald said, but he smiled happily. "But you really should get back to your guests."

"You're right, of course," Alex agreed, tightening his hold on Katherine as he directed her to walk with him toward their formal dining room.

She felt radiant, light, buoyant and not even the slightest bit confused anymore. As they entered the dining room filled with their families and friends, she no longer felt guilt or shame at what they'd done.

The dinner progressed merrily, with guests happily getting to know each other across the huge dining table. Alex sat at the table's head, but he leaned close to Katherine who sat at his right, his elbow resting on the table so he could bend near enough to hear every word she said. He laughed with her, toasted with her, fed her wedding cake. Two minutes before Katherine would have gone to change clothes to throw the bouquet and they would have made an official exit, Ralph caught Alex's elbow.

"I need to see you in the library."

"Now?" Alex asked, his eyebrows arching with incredulity.

Ralph sighed. "Sorry, yes." He turned to Katherine with a smile. "Please excuse us, Mrs. Cane."

It was the first time anyone had called her Mrs. Cane, and the name rolled over Katherine like something akin to a piece of heavy equipment. It left her so stunned and speechless, she let them leave unquestioningly, but it also left her with a desperate need. When she threw this bouquet, when she tried to grace another person in this room with her marital bliss, it would be wonderful to know it was bliss.

Without another thought, she slipped out of the living room and down the hall to the den. The minute Ralph stepped out of the library, she was going to pop in and confess to Alex. Her confession would lead him to make a similar confession, she was sure. And, then, then, they really would be married.

She waited five minutes before her patience waned. Any minute someone would catch her here and drag her back into the party. And she didn't want to go. Not yet. She wanted the charade to be over.

Impatient, she grasped the doorknob, but discovered the door hadn't been tightly closed. She would have jumped back guiltily, but Ralph's words caught her attention.

"Just take a quick look at it. I think you'll like it. I know we all got caught up in the excitement of the wedding, but it's never really too late to get a prenuptial agreement signed." He chuckled. "I modified what you should have had Katherine sign weeks ago, and now it's a postnuptial agreement, but it's still an agreement and it's still valid."

There was a long, pregnant pause wherein Katherine held her breath waiting to hear her husband's answer. In the end, he merely said softly, "Sit down, please, Ralph." Katherine imagined he said that because he was busily reading the document he was about to have her sign.

Sickened, not because of Ralph and Alex, but because she'd been foolish enough to fall in love, Katherine quietly moved away from the door and leaned against the wall beside it. *God, she was so stupid.* Heat poured over her, through her. She'd just about made a complete fool of herself! How could she have been so stupid? She'd been thinking like a high school girl, imagining a few kisses meant a man loved her.

Pushing herself away from the wall, she scampered back to the dining room.

Saved, she thought, grateful that she hadn't embarrassed herself. She ignored the tear that slid down her cheek. She didn't have time to feel sorry for herself.

Or any reason. She'd known exactly what she was getting herself into, and when Alex asked her to sign on the dotted line, she would do it happily, without question, without comment, without remorse.

# *Chapter Nine*

Katherine turned away from the door and slowly made her way up the hall, toward the foyer. Denny met her at the bottom of the staircase.

"What are you doing here, kid?" he asked, then popped a cookie in his mouth. "I thought you'd be upstairs changing clothes so you and Alex could leave."

"Yeah, I'm on my way now."

Denny studied her face intently. "Something wrong?"

Realizing her mood was giving away her distress, Katherine lifted her chin and put a smile on her lips. "No," she said in a light, airy voice. "I guess I'm a little tired."

"Well, don't get too tired," Denny said, then gave her a friendly elbow in the bicep. "You're about to go on a honeymoon."

Just the mention of the honeymoon caused Katherine's heart to stop. She'd almost forgotten about that. Denny didn't see her reaction because he turned and began walking toward the living room again. At the same time, Katherine heard the sound of Ralph and Alex leaving the library.

Not wanting to get caught too close to the library for fear they'd realized she'd eavesdropped...

Worse, not wanting to face them and their prenuptial agreement in front of her guests...

Even worse, not wanting them to realize she was upset and then have Alex pretend to be patronizingly solicitous again...

Katherine lifted the heavy skirt of her velvet gown and began jogging up the staircase. Though she didn't look back and couldn't look back because she was desperately trying to get herself to her room to compose herself, Katherine could have sworn she heard the sound of the front door closing. She paused, remembered that she didn't want to be caught, and continued on her way.

She was hopping into black suede pumps when Alex knocked on her bedroom door. Her gown lay across her bed, waiting for Ronald to handle its cleaning. She'd changed into an emerald-green sheath, purchased specifically for its brilliant color. When she tossed her bouquet, she and Alex would stand on the spiral staircase, surrounded by white walls and bright light from the chandelier. Somehow when she saw the dress, she knew the deep hue was exactly what they needed to add color and drama to the picture for their wedding album. Now it seemed pitiful that she'd hungrily, anxiously, tried to make this wedding real.

"Come in," she called, trying to sound as happy as she had been when they'd parted company after the beautiful gift and a passionate kiss.

"That took a little longer than I expected," Alex said, and immediately caught her by the elbows. It was easy to see that his intention was to stop her long enough to pull her into his arms, but Katherine wasn't going to be fooled again. All along, Alex had been trying to bring her into this relationship on a level that would include sex. After all, wasn't that his modus operandi? Great lover. She'd been the one to confuse real emotion for his genuine lust. Now she would have to be the one to pull them back out again.

"That's okay," she said brightly. "It's not as if I'm a real bride, desperately awaiting the return of her only true love."

"Oh, really?" he said, and this time succeeded in grabbing one of her arms. He spun her around handily and caught her against his chest. "That's not what it felt like in the dining room about twenty minutes ago."

"Spirit of the moment," she answered flippantly and tried to spring out of his embrace, but couldn't. With seemingly effortless movements, he held her prisoner against the hard wall of his chest.

Little pinpricks of delight began to rise along her skin, even as flashes of awareness danced through her brain. Her breasts had been flattened against his chest. His arms felt like steel bands across her back. Their thighs brushed. Their bellies pressed together.

And they felt so damned right.

So damned perfect.

So completely, absolutely perfect.

Katherine actually wanted to weep with despair. If she couldn't see through the antics of a man who didn't love her, only wanted to sleep with her, would she ever be able to recognize true love? If she couldn't tell the difference between love and lust with a man she knew to be less than ethical in the romance department, was she doomed to a life of living alone? And why was it that a part of her didn't want to see through him? Why was it part of her just wanted to grab this happiness and savor it for as long as it lasted? To hell with the pain that would undoubtedly follow at some point down the road.

Katherine drew a long breath and closed her eyes. "Let me go, Alex."

"Why?" he teased.

"Because you're starting to get a little too chummy. I think you're starting to believe your own PR."

She opened her eyes at the precise moment that his face scrunched up in confusion. "What happened to the woman I was talking with before I stepped into the library?"

The mention of the library strengthened her resolve. She lifted her chin and looked him right in the eyes. "Alex, are you expecting anything specific in return for those earrings?"

A slap across his cheek couldn't have gotten a more dramatic reaction. His eyes widened and his jaw slackened until his lower lip fell open. "What, exactly, are you saying?" he asked in a deadly quiet voice that raised gooseflesh on her arms.

Still, she didn't let him see she'd reacted and she didn't back down. "Did you give me that gift, expecting that it would soften me up enough that I'd fall into your arms and be the warm loving bride you think I should be tonight in bed?"

She watched that accusation sink in by degrees. First, it hurt him. Then it made him angry. Then he turned into a complete stranger right in front of her. His facial features hardened, his body stiffened, his eyes seemed to turn a dull, less expressive green.

Bending at the waist, he scooped her overnight bag from beside her bed. "Let's go."

"I want an answer to my question," Katherine persisted, staying right where she was despite the fact that Alex was marching toward the door.

He dropped the overnight bag and pivoted to face her. "Don't worry your pretty little head," he said quietly. "Your virtue is completely safe with me."

"At the expense of my sanity, no doubt," Katherine answered indignantly. "In other words, if I don't sleep with you, you're going to be angry and grouchy for the next eleven years."

He rounded on her once again, but this time his hostility was evident, sitting on the surface of his skin, radiating from him like the light of a gas lamp. "What in the hell do you want?"

"I want a promise."

Mouth agape in disbelief, he said, "What kind of promise?"

"I want you to promise you'll never kiss me again, never touch me again, unless we're around other people and the kiss or the touch is specifically necessary to fulfill our charade."

He stared at her for several seconds, before shaking his head and turning away from her. "Somehow, Katherine, right at this moment that promise is not difficult to make at all."

"Then I have it?" she persisted.

"Have what?" he asked angrily.

"Your promise."

"Lady, you not only have my promise, you have a solemn, gilded-edged vow. Now let's get going."

She grabbed her bouquet and her black suede clutch bag from the edge of her bed and followed him out of the room. He'd walked her overnight bag to the top of the back stairs for a staff member to take to the Mercedes, so by the time he joined her at the top of the staircase, Katherine's mood had returned to as much of a normal mood as she could muster given the circumstances.

Still standing behind the barrier of a wall, Alex took Katherine's elbow. "I'm allowed to do this, right?"

She sighed. "This is exactly the kind of behavior I'd expect from you," she said quietly. "You can't have your own way so you'll torment me for the rest of my life."

"Actually, Katherine," he said, stepping forward with her to put them in the spotlight again, "that's exactly what I was just thinking about you."

The guests had assembled at the bottom of the steps and as Alex made the last of his accusations, he propelled Katherine in front of her audience again. The crowd broke into a comfortable patter of applause as Katherine and Alex made their way down the steps.

The photographer continued to snap pictures as he'd been doing all day long. Katherine forced her lips into a wide, happy smile. When Alex stopped her in about the middle of the spiral staircase, she turned a loving smile at him. A moment, she noted by a flash from above, which was captured for all time. Then she turned, and he turned with her, pressing his chest against her shoulder, as they both leaned over the banister. She supported herself with one hand on the railing. He covered that hand with his own. She tossed the bouquet. He caught her now-free hand and brought it to his lips. She took her gaze from her hand and glanced up at him. He stared at her with a look that was such a combination of regret and longing, that Katherine's heart stopped.

All in all, it felt as if it were happening in slow motion, and for a second Katherine wondered if she hadn't made a mistake. Something in the pit of her stomach expanded until she found it hard to breathe. What was happening between them? Why couldn't they seem to find a common emotional ground and stay there? Why did they keep doing this? Bouncing back and forth between loving and hating each other? Why did they even consider loving each other at all?

The shouts of glee brought Katherine out of her reverie as Denny caught the bouquet; then with the same reaction one would have if they caught a poisonous snake, he bounced it over to Caryn.

Everyone in the room laughed outrageously and, in keeping with the spirit, Katherine turned and smiled up at her husband again. But he wasn't looking at her, he was looking at Caryn. Really looking at Caryn. Studying her as if he were only actually seeing Katherine's gorgeous blond administrative assistant for the first time.

Something burst and exploded in Katherine's chest. She could see Alex and Caryn together. Now, *they* were a match. Neither interested in a commitment, both of them happy to have a good time for as long as it lasted. Both of them outgoing, fun-loving, typically outrageous people. They were perfect for each other.

Just the thought of Caryn and Alex together hurt Katherine to the point that her knees buckled. Caryn and Alex were the match, but Katherine was married to him.

"Let's go," Alex said, nudging Katherine as an indicator that she should start down the steps. Forcing herself out of her disturbing thoughts, Katherine took a quick breath and did as he asked.

Once in the foyer, they met Caryn. She happily threw her arms around Katherine. "Oh, you are going to be so happy."

Katherine cleared her throat. "Yeah."

"And you," Caryn said, and turned her attention toward Alex. She smiled up at him and he smiled down at her and Katherine felt a knife twisting in her chest. "You'd just better make my boss happy," she commanded merrily, then rose to her feet and planted a firm kiss on Alex's smooth cheek.

Katherine watched Alex's eyes open widely, then saw his hands shift upward slightly as if his instinctive reaction to having this beautiful young woman so close would have been to pull her into his arms. He wanted to pull her into his arms. He wanted to touch her.

And he couldn't.

Katherine watched all that register in his face, even as she watched him still his normal reactions, and with them it felt as if her chest caught fire.

If she'd ever thought she'd known jealousy, if she ever thought she'd known pain, Katherine suddenly realized she had been wrong. Because jealousy was a sick, encompassing feeling that left you impotent and destroyed. And pain was the knowledge that you'd made all the wrong moves for all the right reasons and there was no way to back out and no way to fix them. There was no way to change a man like Alex Cane, to make him a family man. To make him faithful.

To make him love her.

To make him love her when he really wanted someone else.

Anyone else.

It didn't have to be Caryn who was kissing his cheek. It could have been anyone. This was a man who didn't merely like women, he was well accustomed to having them throw themselves at his feet.

This episode would be repeated a hundred times over the next eleven years and there would be nothing Katherine could do about it.

If she ever harbored the slightest hope of making him love her, it died right then and there.

Katherine felt as if her dreams were being shattered right before her eyes. She would never pull out of this. Never be the same. She loved Alex with the depth and breadth and height of her soul. But she would never get him to actually love her....

Because he couldn't.

## *Chapter Ten*

At the end of a two-week honeymoon in the Bahamas that could only have been described as a workaholic's dream, Katherine and Alex arrived home tired and frustrated, but the minute they saw Jason all that changed.

He leapt into Alex's arms and hugged Katherine from his perch against Alex's chest. Katherine's parents stood by, both holding back tears.

"He was the best boy," Mary Whitman reported as Richard looked on approvingly. "He didn't give us a minute of trouble."

"Of course, Ronald was always around the corner with some entertainment for those few times when it looked like we might have a problem with boredom," Richard admitted with a chuckle. "But basically, everything went very, very well."

Katherine breathed a sigh of relief. "That's great," she said, even as she noticed out of her peripheral vision that their luggage was being removed from Alex's car. It had been this way from the minute they stepped off the plane on the island. There was always someone available to do Alex's bidding. Not that that was bad, it was merely unusual to a woman who'd spent her entire life doing everything for herself. Though Katherine thought she was getting used to it, seeing it all happen in a different environment reminded her all over again that she hadn't married the boy next door. Alex's life was so incredibly fantasy-like that it actually lent a certain authenticity to the fact that their marriage would be different from what her parents, her friends and even her co-workers would be expecting. Which would actually cover a multiplicity of oddities that would undoubtedly occur because they weren't really in love.

Sighing, she stepped away from Jason and Alex. "Well, if no one minds, I'm going upstairs to change."

"Me, too?" Jason asked suddenly, as if he didn't want to let her out of his sight.

Alex picked up the cue like a pro. "Why don't you spend some time with me while Aunt Kate's gone?"

"No!" Jason cried, almost leaping out of Alex's arms to reach for Katherine.

Holding on to Jason securely, Alex said, "She's going to be changing clothes, sport. That means she'll want to be alone." Without giving Jason the opportunity to protest further, Alex turned to Katherine's father. "Come on, Richard. Let's give the ladies their privacy. We'll take Jason back to the library and you two can tell me all the things you did while I was gone."

"Okay," Richard said, gladly following Alex down the corridor.

Katherine stared after them. There they were, her nephew, her father and her husband, walking down the hall to her library. It was mind-boggling.

As if reading her thoughts, her mother walked over and stood beside her, watching the three men as they made their way down the hall. "Hard to believe, isn't it?" she asked softly.

Katherine swallowed. "Actually, yes."

"You know, Katherine," Mary said quietly, "this all fell together so quickly and so conveniently, that I struggled to believe it was real. But when we were here for your engagement party, you and Alex put all my fears to rest."

Mary paused, catching Katherine's gaze before she continued. "But, right now, I'm just a little bit confused again."

Katherine swallowed. "Why is that?"

"After two weeks of being married, it should have been almost second nature for Alex to settle Jason's tantrum by taking him upstairs with you. He's only two, and I'm sure you have a private bathroom. That's not the first time I've noticed that you and Alex give each other an unusual kind of privacy. Almost as if you're not . . . intimate."

"Well, Mom," Katherine answered easily. "Alex leads a very different kind of life, and we're probably going to have a different kind of marriage than what you're used to seeing—"

Mary stopped her with a slight wave of her hand. "You really don't have to explain to me, dear. But I do want to say for the record that I'd be really disappointed to discover that you'd married Alex for anything less than love."

With that, and without giving Katherine the opportunity to respond, she turned and began walking up the spiral staircase, but she stopped abruptly and faced Katherine again. "So would Jessica, I believe."

Katherine's heart froze in her chest. She knew what was going through her mother's mind. All those problems Jessica had with Alex. All those reasons not to like or trust him. The discovery that Katherine might have married him for anything other than love, had reminded her mother that Alex had a reputation for buying what he wanted. It brought back painful, unhappy memories of an Alex who Katherine was sure no longer existed, and it put Mary Whitman in a position of feeling as if she were betraying a beloved daughter.

Katherine changed her clothes quickly, but then paced her bedroom, not quite sure of what to do. But the answer actually came with relative ease. She and Alex were partners in crime. Part of this charade was to make it believable to everyone. It didn't matter that this was Katherine's mother or that Katherine would be forced to confront Alex with the horrible truth that her entire family hated him for all the years Jessica was married to Ryan. Katherine had to tell Alex what was going through her mother's mind, and then she and Alex had to solve the problem.

Together.

Poking her head out of her bedroom door, Katherine looked both ways down the hall, and once she was sure the coast was clear, she ran down to Alex's room. Without a thought for propriety, she twisted the knob and jumped inside, closing the door behind her.

Pressing her forehead against the heavy wooden portal, she spent a few seconds catching her breath, but the loud sound of someone clearing their throat behind her, caught her attention and she spun around.

"Oh, heavens!" she yelped, when she saw that Alex stood by his bed dressed only in satiny boxer shorts. As quickly as she faced him, she pivoted around again, but nothing could stop the image of his wide, bronze chest, or his long, perfect thighs, as that picture firmly embedded itself in her brain and wouldn't erase.

"Katherine, if you would have knocked, I would have asked you to wait a minute," Alex patiently advised her.

"I couldn't wait. I couldn't risk my mother seeing me knocking on your door. We're supposed to be married, remember?" she asked, her back still facing him.

"Oh, for Pete's sake," Alex groaned, and in her mind, Katherine could see him pinching the bridge of his nose the way he did whenever he realized he'd made a mistake. "Are we stupid or what?"

"I'd like to think we're 'or what,'" Katherine said. "Because we're not stupid. We simply don't have any experience in pretending to be married."

"You can turn around now," Alex said, and once she had faced him again, he continued. He'd slid into a pair of faded jeans but his bare chest still gleamed at her, tempting her with its beautiful masculinity. The thought occurred that she should turn around again, but she swallowed and forced herself to focus on what he was saying.

"I hate to say this, Kate," he said, then pulled a sweater over his head. "But you're going to have to sleep in my room tonight."

She sighed. "Yeah, I know. I figured that out already. We could say my room is more or less a dressing room...."

"No, I think we'd better cover all our bases and have Ronald start moving your things in here." He paused and looked at her. "How long did you say your parents were staying?"

"Only another two days."

"Okay, no point in disrupting everything, but I do think it might not look right unless it at least appears that you're moving in here."

"Okay," she agreed, then licked her dry lips. It was hard, really hard, being in such an intimate setting with him and not imagining what it would be like to really be married to him. To be sharing his life, his house, his bed, for real. Even after two weeks of barely speaking, the idea was so appealing it was almost frightening. Or maybe it was because they'd spent the past two weeks not speaking that the idea held such a ridiculous appeal. She was hungry, so hungry for a decent word from him, a compliment, a stolen kiss. Anything.

It was pitiful.

"Katherine? Is there something else?" he asked patiently.

She drew a long breath. "Alex, my mother suspects that we married for all the wrong reasons."

"Oh-oh," he said, then sat on the bed.

"That would be bad enough," Katherine admitted and walked over to sit beside him. "But you weren't exactly loved by our family."

He peeked over at her. "I know. Even when I was sitting in the library with Jason and your father, I had minutes when I was tempted to pinch myself."

Katherine smiled. "My father really likes you."

"I know he likes that I'm rich," Alex said, but he laughed to cover an unintentional insult.

"He likes your money because to him that's a sign that you're smart, crafty. He appreciates craftiness. He thinks that's the modern-day version of strength."

"And here I only thought he liked drinking good brandy."

Katherine burst into a round of giggles because she could see her father enjoying his nightly snifters by the fire. Richard Whitman had grown quite fond of his new son-in-law's wealth, but in a charming, endearing kind of way.

"Don't be too hard on him," she implored softly, her eyes moving upward to catch his gaze.

Alex glanced down, and when he caught her pleading smile, he bestowed upon her a look of such longing, Katherine almost felt like a real bride, asking for mercy from her real husband. Finally he sighed and looked away. "The last thing I want to be is hard on your father," he said quietly. "I really like the guy. I even like the way he likes my money. It gives us a point of reference, something to talk about. Which is more than a lot of new sons-in-law can say."

Katherine giggled again, and Alex tossed her a crooked smile. "Now, your mother. That's an entirely different matter."

"And that's our problem."

Alex sighed. "Honestly, Kate, I have no idea of what we should do."

Katherine cleared her throat. "Actually, I think I do."

He glanced at her. "You do?" he asked incredulously.

She looked down at her hands. "I think my mother's going to be watching for us to be acting more like newlyweds."

His eyebrows rose. "Really?" he asked, the laughter evident in his voice. "And...uh...how would you propose we fix that?"

"I think you're going to have to start kissing me again."

She said it without looking at him, so it didn't surprise her when his fingers reached out and tilted her chin until he forced her to meet his gaze.

It didn't surprise her when his face bent toward hers. It didn't surprise her when he said, "Like this?" just two seconds before his lips brushed across hers.

His kiss was as sweet as a happy-ending bedtime story, as joyous as a reunion between two long-lost friends, yet it bore an edge of desperation, quickness, need that nudged aside the softness and plunged them into an abyss of sensation that vied for control until it eventually won. Her arms slid around his shoulders. His hands slid down her back, absorbing the feel of her, her form, until the simple exploration didn't seem to be enough and he pulled her forward, crushing her against him.

The bed creaked but the air was punctuated by the sound of desire, two people feeding a hunger that had gone ignored for so long, neither one of them could contain it any longer. They nipped and suckled and touched and explored until, of their own volition, they fell backward on the soft mattress.

The second her head hit the satin of his comforter, Katherine seemed to get her senses back. The feel of him, the scent of him, the need for him intoxicated her, but here they were at the onset of their very first crisis, losing control like two teenagers angry with their parents.

Squeezing her eyes shut, Katherine took a long breath, then pulled away from him. "I don't think we want to go quite so far in front of my mother."

He stopped her when she would have sat up. "Why not?" he asked, smiling in a way that somehow combined devilish intent and a near pleading. "I don't think she'd question our purpose for marrying anymore if we did."

Katherine couldn't help herself, she laughed. "You're supposed to cherish and revere the woman you love, not ravish her before dinner."

She tried to leave again. He stopped her again. "Where do you get this nonsense? The woman I marry will be every bit as much as an object of my desire, as my love. For me the two are somewhat synonymous."

"Yeah, well, just don't show that side of yourself to my mother."

"I still say it would keep her questions to a minimum."

"And I say it would cause her to question my sanity." She stopped and sighed. "Please," she pleaded somewhat humbly, "this is my mother. She thinks I'm pure and spotless. Could we please keep it that way?"

He shrugged. "You're the boss."

This time when Katherine pushed herself off the bed, Alex let her go. But when she was nearly at the door, he called, "Katherine?"

She paused, but didn't turn around. "Yes?"

"*Are* you pure and spotless?"

The question astounded her so much, and held such a huge air of hopefulness, that Katherine faced him. "Would it matter?"

He countered her question with a question. "Does it matter that I'm not?"

She paused a second and actually considered the situation before she said, "Let's not argue over things that aren't relevant, shall we? I think we have enough problems without bringing up things that don't count."

With that she turned and walked out of his bedroom, but once in the hall, she paused to collect herself. If the man didn't kill her with kisses, he would most certainly someday push her to the edge of her control and bring them both to the argument they'd best be avoiding.

Because the problem was, despite the fact that it should matter that he'd been with more women than Katherine had co-workers, relatives and friends added together, it didn't matter. It did at one time, in the beginning, but not anymore. She was desperately, hopelessly in love with him.

But he could never know.

## Chapter Eleven

"Well, I think it's time we turned in for the night."

"Oh, okay, Dad," Katherine said, smiling lovingly at her parents who rose from their seats on side-by-side gingham chairs. They'd gathered in a small sitting room, a room that Katherine had decorated for reading and relaxing. Given that half the area was glass, Ronald used that portion as a greenhouse, but the half that was part of the main house had been empty until Katherine realized it would make a comfortable place for morning coffee. While she and Alex were away, her parents had decided they liked sitting in the room in the peace of the evening, looking at the stars, thinking of the future. Katherine had considered it such a good sign that they were comfortable, able to look at the future again, that she didn't argue when they led everyone to the sun-room sitting area for after-dinner discussions.

"Katherine, aren't you and Alex coming, too?" Katherine's mother asked quietly.

"Actually, yes," Alex said, jumping up from his seat beside Katherine on the blue gingham sofa. He didn't give Katherine the opportunity to argue or agree, merely pulled her up to stand in front of him, then wrapped his arms around her waist from behind and snuggled his chin into her shoulder. "We'll be along as soon as I check all the lights and doors."

The warmth of his arms around her was nothing compared to the fact that she was held tightly against him, feeling his entire body pressed against the back of her entire body. It had been difficult enough pretending she didn't notice or care about his nearness in the beginning of their relationship. But now that she'd seen him swimming in the tropics, sunning himself in a bathing suit that was actually very discreet, but which still exposed most of his beautiful body to her, pretending she didn't notice or care about his nearness was almost impossible.

Despite the fact that he was lean to the point of being thin, Alex had perfect, well-defined muscles, particularly in his chest, which wasn't covered with hair, but rather, bare, sun-bronzed skin that made it possible to see muscle tone and definition. He had a flat stomach, long legs and the buttocks of a man who obviously worked out.

And he was holding her against him right now. Pulling her into all that beautiful structure, those clean lines, that sun-bronzed flesh.

And she fit.

She fit wonderfully, perfectly.

Katherine's parents nodded and began to walk away, and Katherine knew the relief of a woman about to be released from prison, but her father turned around suddenly. "Gee, you know, we always assumed Ronald checked the locks and the lights. We never once did it while you were gone," he admitted guiltily.

"That's okay," Alex said. "I told Ronald to close the house up for the night while we were gone."

"Oh," Richard Whitman said, then turned and walked out of the room.

Katherine let out the breath she didn't realize she was holding and jumped away from Alex as if his shirt were on fire.

"Okay, let's get the doors and lights and get this over with," she mumbled indignantly.

"Relax," Alex said, shaking his head. "Ronald really does lock up for the night. I only created that story to buy us some time before we have to go upstairs."

Katherine's forehead puckered. "Why?"

"So they're asleep, or at least very drowsy when we go upstairs. That way, any inadvertent comment we make won't float through the walls."

"You put my parents in the room next to ours?" Katherine gasped, incredulous.

"*Ronald* put your parents in the room next to *mine,*" Alex said, sighing heavily as if very tired of dealing with the situation. "That was before we were married and before we realized we'd have to share a room tonight."

Katherine cleared her throat to stop an outburst of temper that wouldn't do either one of them any good, particularly since no one was at fault, least of all Alex. Feeling her anger subside, though not actually calm, she asked, "So what do you want to do? Play cards for the next twenty minutes?"

"No. We can probably go upstairs now, as long as we both understand that we can't say anything that will lead your parents to recognize that we're not . . . not . . ."

"Sleeping together?" Katherine ventured quietly.

"Well, we will be sleeping together, just not *sleeping* together."

She would have laughed at the way the notorious Alex Cane had grown so Victorian since their marriage except she had other, more pressing concerns. "What do you mean we will be sleeping together?"

"There's only one bed, and I'm not sleeping on the floor." He paused, considered, then said, "And don't bother volunteering to sleep on the floor yourself. I don't want to run the risk that Jason will wander in in the middle of the night and slip it to your mother that he found you on the floor by the bed."

Visions of sharing a bed with Alex, the sun-bronzed man she'd admired at the beach, made her swallow. "Alex, no," was all she could manage to say.

"No?" he asked quietly.

"You know what I mean."

"Yes, quite frankly I do know what you mean. But I'm tired. Tired from the trip and tired from pretending. But most of all tired of jumping to make *you* comfortable, when we're supposed to be in this together. Believe it or not, *princess,* tonight you won't have a damned thing to worry about."

With that he stormed out of the sun-room and for about thirty seconds, Katherine stood there dumbstruck. Bright stars twinkled overhead. Green plants stood like hearty sentinels. The gingham furniture looked comfortable, homey. Absolutely nothing had changed in the last twenty minutes, yet Katherine felt totally different.

Was she being difficult?

Wasn't she holding up her end of the bargain?

*Was* he jumping to make her comfortable?

Sighing, she fell to the gingham sofa and covered her face with her hands. It almost appeared she'd been so busy protecting herself, she'd forgotten they'd made commitments to each other. They'd made a deal that allowed them both the opportunity to raise Jason. So, why, every time she was in the same room with Alex, did she keep forgetting that she had responsibilities, certain things to do to keep their bargain?

She rose.

She wouldn't forget again.

Careful not to make a sound, Katherine tiptoed upstairs. Ten minutes before that, she would have experienced a certain trepidation in opening the door to Alex's bedroom. Now she grabbed the knob and twisted it as if it were the most normal thing in the world.

When she entered the room, Alex wasn't anywhere to be seen, so she looked around more closely than she had that afternoon at the small, comfortable, simple room.

A dark-colored braided rug covered a hardwood floor. A burgundy, green and black print comforter matched the curtains of the same print, but otherwise the room was without decoration. There were no pictures, no flowers, no statues. It was, quite simply, a place to sleep.

Tension ebbed from the back of her neck. She could do this.

Alex appeared from the bathroom. One hand buffed his hair with a thick peach towel. He wore a forest-green paisley robe and beneath its hem were the legs of a pair of deep green pajamas. She refused to look at the triangle of exposed skin at his throat. Refused to think about the fact that the legs covered by those silk pajamas would be stretched out right beside her all night.

"Oh, I see you've decided to join me."

"And to apologize," she said immediately, pushing all thoughts of him, his beautiful body and her dwindling control to the farthest corner of her mind. She was a grown-up; he was a grown-up. They had a bargain. She had no reason to doubt him, and she herself had self-control the size of the Hoover Dam. They could do this. They had to do this. They both understood the stakes, and because they both understood the stakes, neither would slip.

"You're right. I have been acting like a princess. We are in this together. From now on, I promise to keep up my end."

Alex sighed. "And I apologize for acting like such a bear. I know this is hard for you. I realize it must be difficult to have to convince your parents. But I'm not the enemy," he said, his gaze holding hers. "We are now officially on the same side."

"I know," she whispered solemnly.

"Good."

As casually as if they'd been married for forty years, Alex turned away from her. He deposited his towel in the bathroom, then returned to the bedroom, took up residence on what must be his favorite side of the bed and picked up a book from a bedside table.

Deciding there was nothing left to discuss, Katherine found her own pajamas, which Ronald had stashed in the chest of drawers. She inspected the bathroom and found soap, shampoo and conditioner. She found washcloths, fresh towels and absolutely everything else she needed. With a sigh, she closed the bathroom door and took a shower.

When she returned to the bedroom, Alex was lying down, turned toward the wall. He'd left his reading light on and Katherine used it to direct herself to the bed. Gingerly, she lifted the cover, then slid herself underneath.

Alex never stirred. Katherine drew a sigh of relief. She held herself as stiff as a board and wondered if she'd sleep at all, but at least she would be holding up her end of the bargain.

Actually, physically holding up her end of the bargain.

Holding it so hard and so dearly that her arms ached.

And her back ached.

And her legs ached.

It was absolutely a miracle that she fell asleep....

And a miracle when she awakened feeling as though she were wrapped in a thick, incredibly warm blanket.

No, it wasn't a blanket, it was something like a comfortable cloud....

No, a cloud was too soft. This was strong, hard, warm....

Another kind of warmth moved along her midsection, under the hem of her pink pajama top, in a half-caress, half-petting motion. Something nuzzled her hair. Comfortable, she shimmied backward, pushing herself more deeply into the warmth that seemed to be welcoming her, pulling her in and then wrapping itself tightly around her....

Her eyes sprang open. *Good God! They were snuggling!*

And oh, boy, did it feel good....

No, it didn't. It couldn't! This man was a womanizing creep. She could love him for the things he did and because he was kind to Jason. And she could be attracted to him because he was physically handsome and sexy as all get out. But she couldn't actually give in to this. She *couldn't* like him. She *couldn't* enjoy him. It went against everything she believed in.

She scrambled out of bed and into the heat of a morning sunbeam. "Get up, you fool!"

His eyes struggled open. "What?"

"I said, get up!" Furious, she began to pace. "This is it, this is the last straw."

Slowly, he edged himself up on the bed. "What in the hell are you talking about?"

"You," she thundered. "You groped me while we were sleeping!"

"Shh!" he said, fully awake now and batting his hand for emphasis. "Damn it, Katherine, keep your voice down."

"Don't you 'damn it, Katherine' me," she said, but she whispered. "You did this on purpose."

"I did what on purpose?"

"Putting us in the same bed because you knew the gravity of warm bodies would pull us together."

"The gravity of warm bodies?" he asked, confused. Then he snickered, but his chest began to quiver, and pretty soon a full-blown belly laugh exploded from him. "The gravity of warm bodies?" he said again, this time through hysterical laughter.

"Don't you make fun of me," she said, grabbed her pillow and beat him over the head with it. But that only seemed to make him laugh all the harder, which made her all the more determined to subdue him with her pillow. Finally, in a tangle of arms and legs and bedclothes, he grabbed her waist, threw her on the bed and kissed her soundly.

Huge, spasmodic shivers went through her and when she would have given in, succumbed to the horrible temptation of his mouth and warm body, he pulled away from her.

"This is your family, not mine," he said with a deadly seriousness she wasn't expecting given her interpretation of the mood and the moment. "I swear to God, if I have to pull your fat out of the fire one more time," he added in an ominous whisper, "I'm throwing in the towel. Not only will I tell your parents the truth, but I'll take my chances with Judge Black, as well. Pick up your end of the charade, Katherine, or I'm letting go of mine."

He released her then. Dropped her, actually. Then crawled off the bed and disappeared into the bathroom.

She lay on the bed tingling, wondering how she could be so stupid as to keep forgetting they were in a charade together and wondering why she kept forgetting that she officially killed any attraction he might have had for her on their wedding day. She couldn't understand why she didn't just act her age, remember their differences and keep up her end of the bargain.

When he came out of the bathroom, she considered apologizing again, but chose not to. Alex didn't look very receptive.

When she came out of the bathroom, he was gone.

She found him in the sun-room, eating breakfast with her parents and Jason.

"Good morning," she said, mustering a chipper, happy tone that she didn't quite feel.

"Good morning," everybody echoed in return. Even though their voices were mingled, Katherine picked out Alex's voice and heard the anger.

Her tension climbed a notch.

"Did you sleep well, dear?" her mother asked politely, merely as a way to open conversation, but Alex cleared his throat and Katherine felt her face flame with color.

"I slept very well, Mother," Katherine replied evenly, hating the way everything was going wrong and it was her fault. She felt as if she were on a rocket that was spiraling out of control, and even though she sat at the helm she couldn't quite get herself to push the right buttons.

She forced herself.

"Alex, honey," she said lovingly, causing him to look up, his face displaying complete perplexity. "Would you pass me the toast?" she asked sweetly.

"Only if you come over here and give me a kiss first," Alex replied urbanely.

He was testing her. She knew that. She also deserved it. Feigning happiness that ended up being a good cover for nervousness, Katherine rose from her seat, walked the short—incredibly short—distance to Alex's chair, bent and placed her lips on Alex's. She kept the kiss short and chaste, but on a burst of inspiration, she twisted to more or less hide her next move from her parents, and kissed Alex so hard and so long, she stunned him.

When she pulled away, he blinked up at her.

"How's that for commitment?" she whispered.

He blinked again.

"I keep my promises," she added softly, then moved away from him.

Katherine hadn't even returned to her chair before Ronald appeared in the sun-room. "Mr. Cane, you have a visitor," he announced quietly.

Surprised by his formal tone, Alex said, "Who?"

Ronald glanced around the room as if gauging whether or not to make the announcement publicly, then quietly said, "A George Pyle, sir. He's a private investigator. He claims you hired him."

Alex cleared his throat. "Actually, I did," he admitted as he rose from his seat. "This will only be a minute," he added and began to walk away.

Realizing this was the investigator Alex had hired to check up on his sister, Marissa, Katherine sprang from her chair. "I'm going with you."

Alex stopped her with a warning look. "No, that's okay, *darling*. I'll handle this."

"Oh, no, no, no, dear," Katherine countered with sugar-sweet tones. "Like you said last night, we handle everything *together* now."

Alex blew his breath out on a frustrated sigh, but eventually nodded his agreement. Silently they walked to the library, Ronald leading the way, and just as they would have entered the room, Alex caught her hand and gave it a squeeze. "That's all, Ronald," he instructed. Then he turned to Katherine. "This may not be what we want to hear," he reminded her quietly.

She nodded. "I know, but I'm ready."

## *Chapter Twelve*

George Pyle was an awkward man. Short, round, smoking a fat cigar. Katherine gripped Alex's hand a little tighter.

"Well?" Alex asked simply as they entered the room.

"I found several dummy corporations tied up with your sister's ranch," George announced without preamble, then blew a stream of gray smoke into the air. "It seems that these corporations were created to give the appearance that Marissa and her husband are doing well. But the reality is they're on the brink of bankruptcy."

"My God," Katherine said, feeling faint. If they'd waited another few weeks, she and Alex wouldn't have had to get married.

"But?" Alex asked craftily.

"But I can't quite prove all the connections yet."

Katherine almost breathed a sigh of relief, happy that they had made the right decisions after all; then realized that she had become so embroiled and so confused that she was losing her perspective. The thing to be happy about would be their ability to *dissolve* this marriage, not confirm it.

"So how long until you can make the connections?"

"I may never be able to make the connections. Whoever set this up is damned good."

"Okay," Alex agreed amicably, seemingly referring to some agreement he and George Pyle had made before her entry into the situation. "What's our next move?"

"All I can do is keep digging."

"Then keep digging," Alex agreed.

George smiled a happy, I'm-going-to-be-making-some-big-money-from-this-case smile, inclined his head and left the room.

"What do you think?" Alex asked quietly, after George closed the door.

"I don't know what to think anymore," Katherine admitted.

"Well, whatever Marissa's got up her sleeve, she's going to a great deal of trouble. Creating dummy corporations to hide the fact from the judge that she's going bankrupt is not small potatoes. If nothing else, this proves beyond a shadow of a doubt how much she wants Jason."

"But what could she possibly want from Jason?"

"I have absolutely no idea," Alex said, shaking his head in wonder. "He has no money. He has nothing," Alex added, then glanced over at her and caught her gaze. "Except you and me to protect him. Get ready for the long haul, Katherine, because I know Marissa. One little marriage isn't going to stop her."

"What are you telling me?"

"When we go before the judge next August to request custody, it'll be as a couple."

Katherine swallowed. "I know."

"That means Marissa can't beat us as easily as she thought she could. She's going to have to find a way to make us look like unacceptable parents. To do that, she'll be on our tails every minute, trying to find a flaw." He paused, held her gaze. "*This* is the other shoe you've been waiting to fall. This is our real test. Marissa isn't going to let us steal Jason right out from under her. The quickest, easiest way for her to keep us from doing that will be to prove our marriage is a sham."

Even though Alex paused, Katherine said nothing. He had more on his mind—something serious. She could see it in his expression.

Finally he sighed, turned to her and said, "I just want you to remember that Marissa will always be looking over our shoulders, looking for that way or that means to take Jason from us. At this very moment, she could have a detective investigating us the same way we're investigating her."

With that, he turned and left the room, and Katherine felt oddly insulted. He was keeping something from her. She could understand him holding back in the beginning of their relationship, she could also understand his wariness about getting too immersed in each other's lives, but, dammit, this involved Jason. At the very least this "something" involved the woman who was trying to take Jason away from them and Katherine had every right to know what it was.

Ever since their last meeting with the judge, Katherine realized there was more to this mess than he was telling her. More to this custody battle, more to the relationship between Ryan, Marissa and Alex, more to Alex's need to keep his nephew and more to Marissa's equal or greater need to take him away. She'd let it go, not wanting to get involved in a family squabble, but it suddenly hit her that she was part of this family now. Worse, she and Alex were partners in crime. He had no right to hide *anything* from her. And come hell or high water, she was getting to the bottom of this.

A mixture of curiosity and anger propelled her out of the room, but when she found Alex he was in the sun-room with her parents, Jason on his lap.

She waited for an opportunity to get him alone, but there wasn't a time when he wasn't sitting with her father or playing with Jason, her mother only a few feet away sitting on a bench, leaning against a tree or knitting by the fireplace. All of which only cemented Katherine's belief that he was hiding something from her, almost hiding from her—which set her blood to boiling.

For the first time since their marriage, she wasn't only glad, she was anxious when it came time for bed. In her impatience, she showered first, only to discover that meant she had twenty minutes of pacing time while he took his turn in the bathroom. When she heard the shower stop, she jumped into bed so he wouldn't realize she'd been waiting for him.

Finally, finally, he crawled under the covers and Katherine snapped on the lamp by her side of the bed.

"Alex, what are you hiding from me?"

Not quite lying yet, he shifted on his elbow until he faced her. "Hiding from you?"

"You heard me. I want to know what you're hiding from me."

"About what?"

"About Marissa, about Jason... about everything. All of this," she said, spreading her arms out to gesture around the room.

He opened his mouth to answer, but she silenced him by putting her index finger over his smooth lips. "No lies," she warned quietly. "No half-truths. I want the whole story."

"Katherine," he said, then shook his head as if confused. "I'm not quite sure what you want to hear."

"Well, then, why don't we start with you telling me why you want to raise Jason?"

He looked at her. "I've explained that to you."

"Yeah, but you haven't told me the truth. Not the real truth. Not the whole truth. I know your new television station is part of it, but only part. The other half is personal. I saw that on your face this morning. That's what I want to know."

He didn't hedge or falter. Instead, he put his head on his pillow and said, "You're right. The television station was a convenient cover. The truth is, I want to raise Jason to make up for the mess I made of Ryan's life."

"The mess you made of Ryan's life?"

"Oh, don't give me those big eyes and dimples," Alex said, sighing as he leaned over and switched off the bed lamp, blanketing them in total darkness. "You know what I mean." His arm brushed across her breasts. The scent of shampoo and warmth enveloped her. Suddenly she got the strangest sense that it was right, the most natural thing in the world for them to be lying in bed, talking like a long-time married couple.

She sprang up and clicked on the light again. Not only did she want to break the mood, but she certainly wasn't letting him get away with that answer. "I know what I think you mean, but I want a clarification."

He sighed. "Now?"

"Right now."

He sighed again. "I'm not so naive that I didn't realize that the reason Jessica hardly let me see Jason after Ryan's death was because she was mad at me for ruining her marriage by providing Ryan with so many toys and so many flying assignments that he was never home.'' He paused, blew out a long breath, then said, ''I also figured out that she blamed me for Ryan's death. Maybe even your whole family did. Not merely because I bought him the plane, but because I encouraged his life-style. About a month before Jessica died, I saw her point. I saw the truth. I spoiled my brother so much that he never owned up to his responsibilities and because of that, Jason will never know his real father.''

Somewhat shocked by his complete honesty, Katherine cleared her throat. ''I'm sorry to say this, Alex, but you're not going to get an argument from me on that one.''

Alex expected her to say something like that, but her attitude nonetheless infuriated him. To her, life was always simple. Black and white. She had no concept of shades of gray.

''Do you have any idea how hard this has been for me? How difficult it is to know that I'm the person who bought the plane that killed my own brother—my only brother? I wanted him to have the freedom I had, to have as much of the good things that he wanted, things we didn't have as kids. And though I was smart enough to temper my own enthusiasm, to not overdo the entertainment and even to make something of my life in spite of all the money, I wasn't smart enough to notice that Ryan wasn't following suit.''

''I'm not saying that you should have tried to stop him,'' Katherine gasped, scooting up on the bed until she was sitting—in the lit room, dressed only in lightweight pink pajamas.

But Alex didn't notice. In fact, he kept on talking as if he hadn't heard her protest. Driven by demons he sincerely doubted Katherine could understand, he tried to make some sense of a senseless tragedy. Or at least take the blame. If he could take the blame, take responsibility, then he could fix it. He knew he could. He always had.

"I never saw. I never caught him. It never dawned on me to really look at his life and notice or care that he didn't have a job except jobs I gave him, that he was deserting his family, that...that he was going to kill himself."

The sad, almost desperate tone of his voice caused Katherine to reach for his hand. "It wasn't your fault that he died," she said and edged over to get a little closer, to offer a little human comfort. She still held his hand. She took it with her as she nudged herself against his side.

"Of course it was my fault," Alex argued angrily. He pulled his hand out of hers and tried to shift away from her. "I gave him everything he wanted, let him act like some kind of juvenile delinquent, then bailed him out one step ahead of when the repercussions of his actions would have kicked in." He stopped, shook his head. "He was dead before I understood that spoiling him hadn't merely killed him, it had kept him from facing his responsibilities as a husband and a father. So he'd never really had a life. His family hadn't known him. His son never will. And I'm sorry," he said, slapping his open palm on the satin comforter. "Sorry about all of it. Sorry about the trips to Africa and Ireland. Sorry about treasure hunting and exploring and just plain taking him away."

Katherine edged over again, closing the space he'd made between them. "You know, Alex. The one thing all of us—Jessica included—seemed to have forgotten is that Ryan was a grown man. Almost forty when he died. You weren't exactly *supposed* to be his keeper."

"No, but I was his facilitator. Without me he wouldn't have had the money or the 'toys' to do half the things he did."

"You can't take the blame for Ryan's death," Katherine whispered.

"But I have to," he said and bounded out of bed. "Don't you see? I have to."

"But you can't. And I'm not going to let you."

He turned on her then, his green eyes wild and furious. "*You* don't have any say about it." With that, he grabbed his pillow and a blanket from the bed, spun away from her and bounded into the bathroom.

For a few seconds, Katherine sat awestruck, not quite sure what had happened. She'd never seen Alex angry before, particularly not with himself. He was usually so pleased with everything he did that blaming himself for Ryan's death completely baffled her. She lay down and snuggled into her pillow, determined to give him a half hour or so of private time before she went in and tried to continue the discussion, but she fell asleep waiting for him.

The sound of him rummaging through his drawers the next morning awakened her.

Stretching, as she sat up, she said, "Alex?"

"Yeah, Kate, it's me," he said and glanced at her through the mirror. "I'm sorry."

"That's okay. I wanted to get up anyway." She wanted to continue their discussion from the night before, but she knew a wise person wouldn't jump right in without at least a little time to get the sleep out of her eyes and cobwebs out of her brain.

"No, that's not what I meant. I'm sorry about yelling at you last night."

She shrugged. "You don't have to be sorry for how you feel."

He turned away, busying himself with the contents of his drawers again. "Maybe not, but I didn't want to burden you with my troubles."

She smiled. "I am your wife."

It was the first time she'd said it and Alex felt an odd shifting. Trying to sleep on the bathroom floor, he'd come to realize that painful though the admissions were, they'd had a cleansing effect. He knew it wasn't merely because he'd made them aloud, but because he'd made them to someone who genuinely cared about him. He didn't even think Katherine realized it yet, but she cared about him. People like Katherine cared about everybody. They were perfect, soft, wonderful creatures who loved small children, puppies, kittens and cubs, and got along with the neighbors no matter who they were. He supposed that's why it always made him feel so awkward when she made it perfectly clear that she didn't *want* to care about him. He also supposed that right now she couldn't help herself. He might not be a child, a puppy, a kitten or a cub, but spending so much time together over the past several months, one could consider them neighbors.

"Does any of this have anything to do with why you and Marissa don't associate?" Katherine asked.

He shook his head. "No. Marissa made that choice."

"But why?"

He thought for a minute about whether or not he should reveal this last item, then decided he might as well. For as much as he wanted Katherine to like him, to respect him, to appreciate him, he also realized it didn't matter how much she liked him unless she knew the complete truth about him—and like him in spite of it. Which she couldn't do. She might not think all these things would bother her, but someone like him truly didn't fit into her black-and-white, nearly perfect world. It was time they both faced it. "We aren't really family."

"But the judge..."

"The judge made the mistake Marissa's father wanted everybody to make. He assumed I was Judson Cane's son. The truth is my mother was pregnant when she married Judson. I'm not his son. My mother told me that the day before she died. That means I'm not really Jason's uncle, not Ryan's half brother. Hell, I'm not Marissa's half brother. She would be using that against me in court right now if her father and my mother hadn't put his name on my birth certificate. And Judson's dead so they can't do blood or DNA testing to prove the birth certificate wrong, but Marissa was old enough to figure out what happened. And though she can't prove it, she refused to associate with me."

"That doesn't explain why she refused to associate with Ryan."

"Ryan refused to associate with her." Alex paused. He sat beside her on the bed, debating whether or not to continue, then, gentling his voice, unwittingly pleading Ryan's case, he said, "Katherine, when my mother died, Marissa fought to keep me out of inheriting any of the estate. Our family wasn't wealthy, but Judson had a small farm when he married my mother, and my mother had absolutely nothing. In fact," he said, then cleared his throat, "we were very deep in debt. So when my mother died, Marissa tried to keep me from inheriting anything."

"Is she nuts or is she greedy?"

Alex smiled and Katherine began to relax. Alex didn't have a flaw, but through no fault of his own he had a flawed past. And it caused him pain. Real pain. The kind of emotion she didn't think Alex was capable of feeling.

"I think she's a little of both. Anyway, Ryan told her to shove the estate, to keep it, rather than drag the family through that hassle, and he stuck by me. That was when I knew certain ties are stronger than blood ties."

"And why you gave Ryan anything and everything he wanted whenever you prospered."

"I sometimes think Marissa's the reason I got rich. She motivated me into being the best, into being *something* anyway. I suppose it's the seed of opportunity in every adversity theory."

"I've never heard that one."

He rose from the bed, awkward and uncomfortable. She hadn't reacted poorly to the news about him, but after a little time for everything to sink in, she wouldn't be so amiable. She would be as uncomfortable as he was. And he didn't want that. He would much rather have eleven years of pretending to be happy, than eleven years of her avoiding him. "I've got plenty of books by Napoleon Hill. You can start reading right after breakfast."

Knowing he was done talking, sensing his discomfort and willing to pick up this conversation another time, Katherine said, "Pass," then nestled into her pillow again. "I have only one free Saturday every week, but I've got eleven whole years to raid your library."

"Not if Marissa has anything to say about it. There's no way she'll let her bastard brother have anything, absolutely anything that's property of the Canes. And that includes Jason."

## *Chapter Thirteen*

Alex's words resounded in Katherine's head for weeks. Their ominous finality was actually frightening. In the end, she didn't merely understand what he'd told her, she also clearly understood why he had always been so serious about making her fulfill her commitment to their bargain. Why he risked the kisses, inundated her with presents, gave parties. The judge was only a part of the problem. Their real nemesis was Marissa, a woman who would use any means available to hurt Alex.

Consequently, when Alex bought Katherine a string of pearls for Christmas, she not only accepted them with grace, but wore them to work and bragged about them. Bragged about her husband, about her life, about how happy she was.

When Alex took her to New York and decided it was time to update her wardrobe, she allowed him to do so, knowing that the wife of a very wealthy man would happily, automatically accept a new wardrobe.

By the time he bought her the Jaguar as a valentine present, leaving it parked in the lot of her office building for all the world to see, she wasn't merely ready for his generosity, she didn't even question why he'd given the gift publicly. They were trying to convince the world they were happy. Since she'd been in Denver for the past three days, it was more romantic to have the car waiting to be the first thing that greeted her upon her return, than to hold back until she arrived home from work.

After delightedly receiving the keys from Denny, who'd been entrusted with the task of giving them to Katherine the second she entered the building, Katherine allowed a few of her co-workers to accompany her to the parking lot where they all inspected the tiny red sports car. Then, realizing that any wife would rush home to thank her new husband for such a wonderful gift, she shooed her friends away and left work for the day—even though it wasn't even ten o'clock yet.

Katherine screeched her sports car to a stop in front of the five-vehicle storage building, too big, too warm and too clean to be called a garage, and excitedly jumped out of her car. She knew this was a pretend marriage and a sort of pretend valentine's gift, but driving the car to the house had filled her with enthusiasm she hadn't felt since Jessica died. She was bursting to thank Alex for giving her something more precious than a mode of transportation. This wildly extravagant car wasn't merely a statement of luxury. It was *red.* Bright. Beautiful. Full of energy and fire. Exactly what she needed to give her the boost of enthusiasm that told her they could beat Marissa. In fact, she felt the two of them could probably beat anybody.

For that, and the hundred other little ways he'd helped her get through the past few difficult months, Katherine desperately wanted to thank him.

She darted past the garage to the door leading to the breezeway, where she didn't even pause. She slid her key into the door's lock and entered the kitchen.

Still anxious and excited, she ran through the house, not stopping to set her briefcase down or even take off her coat. Instead, she jogged up the circular stairway and, without thought, burst into Alex's bedroom.

Her sudden entry awakened the bed's occupant, and when blond hair appeared from beneath the folds of the covers, not the sandy brown she expected, Katherine's feet weren't the only things to stop. Her heart stopped, as well. The sleeper sat up, revealing quite clearly that she was a woman, a beautiful blond woman who, by the look of the curves beneath the blanket, was incredibly well endowed.

Katherine drew a sharp breath. The pain that shot through her chest felt like a small explosion. "Who the hell are you?" she asked without thinking.

The blonde smiled sleepily. "Sabrina. Who the hell are you?"

Mouth slightly agape, Katherine blinked rapidly. Then, realizing she wouldn't get any answers from this woman and neither did she want answers from this woman, Katherine turned on her heel and exited the bedroom. She couldn't believe this. Absolutely, positively couldn't believe this. Here she was, ready to thank Alex for holding up both their ends of the bargain while she'd been mourning her sister, and she comes home to discover he hasn't been keeping up his own end of the bargain, let alone both of theirs. It was no wonder he'd given her a car. A guilty conscience would do that to a man.

Furious, she yanked off her coat and tossed it to the pole at the bottom of the spiral staircase, then slid her briefcase to the floor where it continued onward until it stopped just shy of the front door. With her hands free and her coat removed, she had no idea what to do next. Then as if by magic, Alex and Jason appeared from the hallway leading to the library.

"Kate!" they both cried excitedly, but Katherine stiffened.

Jason reached her first and wrapped himself around her knees. She gave him a hug. "Hi, honey," she said quietly, and as calmly as she could muster. "How are you?"

"We slept in tent last night."

"You did?" Katherine asked distractedly. "That's wonderful. Look, why don't you do Aunt Katherine a favor and run out to the kitchen and see if you can find Ronald. When you find him, ask him to make me some bacon and eggs, and you help him."

Beaming happily, Jason nodded up at her, then dashed around her and into the kitchen calling for Ronald.

"Something's wrong," Alex said immediately, having seen right through her ploy though Jason hadn't.

"Oh, whatever gave you that idea?"

"Well, your upper lip is puckered for one. But secondly, you don't eat breakfast, so I can tell you're furious about something."

Even as he said the last, he seemed to remember the reason she might be angry, and he grimaced. "Okay, I get it. You're about to scream at me royally." He glanced down the hall, toward the kitchen where Jason had just run. "And that door's not a whole hell of a lot of protection when you decide to break the sound barrier, so let's go into the library."

Deciding to handle this with the dignity that had been her hallmark before grief and confusion had turned her into a woman she didn't even recognize, Katherine straightened regally. "I couldn't agree with you more."

They walked down the hall in silence, but the minute he closed the door, Alex said, "I have an explanation."

"An explanation," she said, whirling to face him, her hope for dignity flying out the window at his flippant attitude. "There is no excuse for blatantly carrying on an affair! You're supposed to be the one who knows how villainous your sister is, but look at you. You're behaving as if you don't care whether or not she's watching! And then there's me. How the hell do you think I feel? And Jason! For God's sake, Alex, what about Jason? How dare you expose him to your little trysts!"

Alex stood perfectly still, looking at her as if she were crazy. "I was about to explain why I bought you the car. I thought that's why you were angry. But this doesn't sound like a discussion about me buying a gift you consider too extravagant. So what in the hell are you talking about?"

"Oh, you think you're so clever," she said, spinning away from him. "But you missed one important thing. You never realized I'd be happy to get this gift, finally accustomed to your extravagance. So you never guessed I couldn't let even an hour go by without thanking you for the beautiful car and that I'd arrive home before you had a chance to get that floozy out of your bed."

"What floozy?"

Furious now, she felt her temperature rise. "The ditsy blonde in your bed!" she shouted. "What do you think I am, stupid?"

"I think you're hallucinating. Jason and I slept in a tent in the basement last night. And we slept in. That's why we're both in sweat suits!"

"Yeah, right," Katherine said, as the library door came open.

"Uh, excuse me," the blonde woman said sheepishly. She wore one of Alex's robes and her feet were bare. "If this is about me sleeping in your bed, I'm real sorry."

"Sabrina!" Alex called delightedly. "Sabrina, honey," he said and very boldly walked over to her and gave her a bear hug and a smacking kiss on the cheek. "When did you get here?"

"About three in the morning. I didn't even wake Ronald. I used my own key and sacked out in the first empty bedroom I found."

Katherine's pulse began to hammer again and the anger in her veins felt hot and impatient. She really, really wanted to shake Alex, and it scared her. She'd never felt this kind of emotion before, never wanted to shake some sense into anyone at the same time that she wanted to beg them to love her. But here it was. The overwhelming sense of passion so hot and so intense that she couldn't tell where the love side of it ended and the hate side began.

"Katherine," Alex said, but his voice came out in a teasing singsong. "This is my cousin. She's a newspaper reporter and was on assignment when we got married, but she's the cousin I wanted to invite to the wedding."

"Uh, now that we have that straightened out," Sabrina said, backing toward the door, "I'd also like to mention that I visited Marissa last week."

Alex gasped a quick, "You did?" but Katherine said nothing. It took all her concentration and energy to breathe.

"Yeah, I tricked her into admitting that she doesn't really want Jason."

"I know she doesn't," Alex admitted cautiously. "I think she's only doing this to keep me from having Jason."

"No, actually, that's not it," Sabrina said, then shrugged carelessly. "I told her I'd like to help her with her custody case for Jason and asked her what kind of dirt she wanted me to try to dig up to help her along. That's when she told me she really doesn't want Jason. She wants money. Lots of money, Alex. In fact, she asked me to deliver the message that if you'd come up with something like three million dollars, she'd be more than happy to drop her appeal of the judge's order granting temporary custody to Katherine. By the way, it's nice to finally meet you," she said, glancing at Katherine with a sheepish smile.

"Three million dollars?" Alex asked incredulously. "She's doing this for money?"

"Well, she thinks she is," Sabrina countered. "Actually when I left her I told her that I figured you wouldn't stand for blackmail, and that you'd probably fight it out with her." Sabrina paused, blew her breath out on a sigh. "That's when she got kind of ugly. I had to admit that if subpoenaed, I'd be forced to testify at the custody hearing about all the things she told me—especially the blackmail part—which would basically blow her good mother act right out of the water."

At that, Alex laughed heartily. "Sabrina, you're bad."

"No, Marissa's bad. I simply play her game as well as she does. Anyway, I think you're off the hook. If you're not, I've got copies of some very interesting financial statements, which prove she's insolvent as hell and can't afford to raise the kids she's got, let alone to add another. I just happened to find them in the safe of her library."

"You stole them?" Alex gasped.

"Didn't have to. She has a copy machine in her library. So I actually didn't steal anything. And the way I look at this, having that copy machine sitting out like that, she was actually inviting me to copy anything I wanted."

Alex laughed heartily, then said, "Sabrina, I could kiss you."

Sabrina smiled. "Save it for your new bride." She turned and began to walk out of the library, but changed her mind and faced Katherine again. "Nice car, by the way. I saw it from the bedroom window."

She left the room unobtrusively, but Katherine hardly noticed. She hated to admit it, but her relief over Sabrina's news about Marissa was nothing compared to her relief over the true identity of the mystery woman in Alex's bed. The sensation of release was so intense, so pure, Katherine nearly fainted. But the burst of release also made her realize she really did love Alex and she couldn't handle the pretense anymore. Especially the pretense of pretending she didn't care about him, didn't love him. Because she did. She loved him.

"I'm glad that..." Alex began, but Katherine turned to face him, biting her lower lip. Her heart hammered, her soul hurt. She couldn't go on like this anymore. One way or another, she had to end the pretense today. But she couldn't do that until she knew how he felt about her.

"Alex, do you care about me at all?" she asked, her voice shaking with the intensity of her emotion.

She watched Alex stiffen. "Katherine, it was a simple mistake. You needn't lecture me. You shouldn't have yelled at me in the first place without the facts."

"I wasn't going to lecture you. I asked if you care about me."

He turned away. "Of course I care about you," he replied airily. "We've been living together for the past three months and seeing each other every day for over half a year, and you're Jason's aunt. Of course I care...."

She drew a long breath, then swallowed. From the man who wanted to ravage her the day after their honeymoon, those few words spoke volumes. "Thank you. I suppose I needed to hear that," she said, then marched toward the door.

Alex caught her hand but she jerked free. "Katherine! Katherine!" he called, running up the hall after her. "Come on, now. What's all this about?" he asked as he followed her.

She didn't say anything, simply plucked her coat from the pole and slid into it.

"Katherine," he said, his tone something akin to a warning. "Okay, look, even though that whole mess was nothing but a mix-up, I can understand your being mad because what you said was all true. Jason shouldn't be exposed to that kind of behavior. But worse, we really would lose him if I were so flippant about my love life. So I understand your getting mad. But now that you understand nothing happened, absolutely nothing happened, you don't have any right to be mad anymore."

Katherine faced Alex. "I'm sorry I overreacted," she said quietly. "That wasn't merely foolish, it was uncalled for, but it also has very little to do with why I'm leaving."

"Leaving?" he asked quietly, cautiously.

"I'm leaving. With Marissa out of the way, we don't really have a custody problem anymore and I can't see any reason to stay."

*Ask me to stay,* she begged in her thoughts, desperately trying to transmit the message to him, even as she desperately tried to walk out of his life with her dignity. He had to make the first move. If she gave him the slightest inkling of how she felt, it wouldn't count because he'd always wanted the sexual end of the relationship, and he would say anything to get that. He had to want her. *Her.* And the only way she would know that he did would be if he would ask her to stay now, when there was no benefit, no reason for her to stay except that they wanted to be together.

"I know that I have temporary custody until August," she said calmly, fighting the sense of grief that threatened to consume her because he wasn't saying anything. Not one damned word. "But I'm willing to go into an informal shared custody agreement with you now, which we can formalize with the judge this summer."

"You're leaving and you're taking Jason?" he asked quietly.

"There's no reason to continue the charade," she stated honestly, giving him that one last chance to realize that all he had to do was ask her to stay, tell her he wanted her to stay, tell her he cared about her even an iota above how much he cared about the other people in his life, but he said nothing. Just stood still and silent by his long, elegant banister, in the echoing foyer. "But you'll have him every day I travel and two weekends a month, if you want. In fact, I'm going to leave him here today if you don't mind, because I need to open my house. I'll call Ronald and tell him to bring Jason once I have the dust covers removed and the heat turned up."

She took a long breath and looked at his beloved face. He still said nothing, merely stared at her. There wasn't a shred of emotion on his face. Though she might have taken comfort from the fact that his lips weren't pulled into their usual grin, his clear green eyes haunted her. If he were sad, or upset, she'd see it. Instead, she saw nothing. "Goodbye, Alex. I'm really sorry this didn't work." *More sorry than you'll ever know,* she said to herself, then turned and walked out the door, knowing that she'd be back here a million times with Jason or for Jason and because of that she'd spend her life connected to a man she loved, but who would never love her.

## *Chapter Fourteen*

Katherine swept her hair into a neat chignon with loose, curly tendrils highlighting her slim neck, but just as quickly she decided it looked perfect, she took it down.

That was the way Alex liked her hair, so she couldn't wear it to the first function at which she would see him in over a week.

Oh, he'd called. He'd called several times. Once she'd even answered her line because Caryn was away from her desk, but Katherine simply told him there was nothing to talk about now that Marissa was out of the custody picture. She didn't go into the explanation of how he'd broken her heart. Because he hadn't broken her heart. If anyone was responsible for the misery she was experiencing right now, it was Katherine herself because she *let* herself fall. No one pushed her.

Sighing, she took a critical look at her simple black crepe sheath. The pearls had been her Christmas gift from Alex, but she wanted to wear them anyway. Their relationship had been the brightest, best thing to ever happen to her and in some respects she wanted to remember it fondly. Despite the fact that he didn't love her, he'd been the best friend she'd ever had. And there was a lot of good in that. Good she could think about on cold winter nights. Good that would keep her company when she was feeling all alone.

Satisfied that she looked nice without looking overdone and without looking as though she wanted to get Alex's attention, Katherine left her home. She'd kept the Jaguar only because Alex refused to take it back. She'd taken it back to the dealer, who promptly delivered it to her home again. So she'd taken it back and he brought it to her home, and she took it back and he brought it to her home....

Realizing they'd go on like that forever, and also, that Alex had enough money he probably didn't miss even the price of a car, Katherine simply kept it. She'd called Munro and asked him to set up a payment schedule. She would be paying on it until the next century, but at least she wouldn't owe Alex anything.

So for now, knowing that they'd both be at this fundraiser since it was an event sponsored by the political party that backed legislation for Alex every time he needed new, improved or altered regulations, and since she needed to attend to attract business for Penn American, even as she kept the local politicians on her side, Katherine hadn't overdressed, or underdressed. She used the car. Wore his pearls. Very soon visitation schedules would be drawn up, and she and Alex would have to see each other again. Part of what she was doing now was an attempt to get herself adjusted to acting normally around him; and the other part was pure torture.

When she arrived at the hotel parking lot, Katherine's heart tripped out a beat that was painfully familiar, but she slid out of her car anyway. She deposited her simple wool coat at the door, smiling as she thought of how Alex probably would have seen to it that her favorite black wool coat would be the next thing from her wardrobe to go. Then she straightened and put on a happy, yet professional smile as she stepped into the banquet room.

Denny met her immediately. "Great party," he sarcastically whispered in her ear.

"Looks divine," she agreed with equal quiet and equal sarcasm.

"I swear, if I could do away with one part of my job this would be it."

"Oh, come on, are you trying to tell me you don't like refried, frozen stuffed mushrooms?"

He glared at her, then glanced around. "By the way, where's your husband?"

Katherine drew a soft breath. "Um, I don't know," she said noncommittally. "I guess he's here somewhere."

"Yeah, well, I'm going to go look for him. He's more fun than these old stuffed shirts. You, on the other hand, should get out there and look for trash."

"Aye, aye," she said happily, jauntily saluting him.

"Just get going," he commanded, then disappeared into the crowd.

Katherine breathed a sigh of relief. Denny would look for Alex for a good half hour before he actually came and questioned Katherine again. By that time, if she was lucky, either she would be busy with a potential customer or Denny would be in conversation with a potential lawmaker, or he'd find Alex and Alex wouldn't embarrass himself by saying anything in public about their breakup.

She had a glass of wine and met representatives from two different companies whose residual waste contracts were about to expire with their present haulers. She gave them cards, gave them pertinent information, then gave them the hard sell and actually believed she'd have both contracts before the end of the month.

Proud of herself, she glanced around for Denny so she could brag, but her eyes collided with the back of a black jacket and her heart stopped. The back was the size and shape of Alex's back. Her gaze jumped higher and when she saw blond hair, not brown, pain squeezed her heart. She didn't know whether she was happy or disappointed the man wasn't Alex, and that disturbed her even more. She was beginning to think that living without him was harder than living with him. The only thing that kept her sane was work, so she looked around for Denny or another customer and eventually found both. But at eleven, the strangest thought hit her. Alex was not in attendance and by then it was so late, she suspected he wouldn't attend.

The same thing happened in a neighboring county the following Thursday. She dressed well and carefully, decided on good excuses they could use in case they were confronted by someone who saw them arrive in different cars, and then she spent the night watching the door for a man who never arrived. When he missed the Saturday morning Rotary breakfast, Katherine began to get nervous. She left the meeting early, and when she stepped into her quiet and cold living room, the phone was ringing.

She grabbed it. "Hello?" she asked anxiously.

"Mrs. Cane?" Ronald asked casually, but Katherine heard the odd tone in his voice and she slowly sank to her sofa.

"Yes, Ronald, what is it?"

He cleared his throat. "I'm sorry to trouble you, madam, but we have a little problem here, and I think you might want to come over this morning...."

"Oh, Ronald," Katherine said, slipping out of her pumps and kicking them beside her stairway. "I can't come over every time something goes wrong."

"You may wish to make an exception this time, Katherine," he argued softly. "You see, I'm leaving."

"You're leaving?"

"I'm sorry, Mrs. Cane, but that's all I wish to discuss about the matter. I wouldn't even have phoned, except I don't believe Mr. Cane can care for Jason in his present condition."

# *Chapter Fifteen*

Katherine still had the key to Alex's magnificent home. After glancing at it guiltily, she slid it into the lock and let herself into the foyer. Jason must have heard the little noise she made because he burst through the door leading to the kitchen. In his haste, his socks connected with the shiny marble floor and he slid the last ten feet and slammed into her legs.

"Jason, honey," she said, stooping to his height as she pulled him into her embrace. "Slow down. Are you all right?"

He nodded vigorously. "Yeah," he said. "Uncle Alex sick."

"Well, I'll go talk with Uncle Alex in a minute, but first I want to make sure you're okay."

He smiled at her and though his grin was much smaller, and held a hint of innocence, he looked so much like Alex that Katherine's heart twisted painfully. "I'm okay," he answered. "Uncle Alex sick," he said again, still grinning sheepishly.

"Okay, Uncle Alex is sick," Katherine said, confirming to Jason that she understood. "Now, where's Ronald? Did he leave already?"

"Uncle Alex yelled," Jason said, his green eyes growing round and huge at the memory.

Katherine frowned. "At Ronald?"

Jason nodded.

"And Ronald left?"

Jason nodded again.

"Okay," Katherine said, letting Jason slowly slide to the floor. "You go into the family room and get out a coloring book. I'll be in to see you in a minute."

"No. Me, too," Jason said, grabbing Katherine's hand and pulling her in the direction of the corridor that led to the library. "Uncle Alex sick."

"You can't go, Jason," Katherine said, and turned him toward the family room again. "Aunt Katherine needs to go alone," she said, glancing down the hall and realizing Jason wouldn't have led her that way if Alex wasn't there.

Jason let out a yelp and tears pooled in his eyes, but Katherine wasn't persuaded to change her mind. "You know better, Jason. When I tell you you can't do something I have good reason. So you go into the family room and I'll get back as soon as I can."

Angry, Jason pushed at her from behind, again in the direction of the library. "Go now."

The expression of real urgency in Jason's voice caused Katherine to turn hastily and rush back down the hall, not quite sure if he wanted her to go immediately so she could get back to play, or if something dreadful was wrong with Alex. He kept saying his Uncle Alex was sick and though Katherine hadn't deliberately avoided that topic, she hadn't really acted as quickly as she could have either. Jason might have gotten so hyper because he thought she was ignoring Jason's two-year-old version of telling her she should have been checking on Alex, not him.

The closer she got to the library door, the more her heart pounded against her ribs. Her own fears pricked her nerve endings, scaring the wits out of her with possibilities, as she pushed open the library door.

She wasn't quite sure what she was expecting to see or find, but when she saw Alex her heart began to beat double time. Sitting with his back to the door, and his feet propped on the windowsill behind the desk, Alex held a glass of something brown and very alcoholic looking in his outstretched hand, which rested on the chair's arm. At eleven o'clock in the morning, he still wore his robe.

"Are you trying to scare the wits out of our nephew?" she asked angrily.

He turned to look at her, but left his feet where they were. He stretched so far, Katherine worried he'd fall out of his chair. But the fact that he could keep his balance was actually a blessed confirmation that he wasn't so sick or drunk, or both, that she should worry about him.

"What?"

"I asked you if you're trying to scare the wits out of Jason. Good Lord, Alex, Ronald called me this morning to tell me he was leaving—and Jason..." She stopped. Her heart still slammed against her ribs, because the rush of relief that registered when she saw that he wasn't ill had been replaced by a wave of desire that took all the adrenaline from her fear and swirled it into the stimulation of need. Even unshaven and wearing a bathrobe, he looked wonderful. In fact, Katherine would almost venture to say he looked better than she'd ever seen him. He had a sort of brooding lord-of-the-manor quality that lent him a lethal sex appeal.

Shaky, half from the residuals of her fear and half from the god-awful fight she had with desire, she took the seat across from his desk.

"I think I'm going to have to kill you."

"Oh, yeah?" he said, then sort of toasted her with his drink. "Right now I'm not sure I'd put up too much of a fight."

Glancing at the glass, which she strongly guessed to be holding bourbon, her eyes narrowed. "Where were you Thursday?"

He shrugged. "Here. Where should I have been?"

"At a fund-raiser. It was for one of your friends, remember?"

He blew his breath out on an unconcerned sigh. "Big deal."

"What is the matter with you?"

He swung his feet to the floor, then rose from his seat. "Will you please leave me alone? I just want to be alone."

His attitude infuriated her. "You self-centered, self-serving, obnoxious idiot," she said, slapping her clutch bag on his desk. "To think I came running back here because I thought you were sick. But all you are is rude."

"Your mistake."

"Oh, yeah," she said angrily. "I can see it was a mistake to be concerned enough to come and check on you."

"Let's get something straight here," he scoffed. "You didn't come out here because you were concerned about me. You checked up on me for Jason's sake. You are, after all, still his sole legal guardian."

She drew a quick, insulted breath.

"Oh, don't pick now to get all sanctimonious on me," he continued angrily. "It was *you* who chose to desert *me*, despite our agreement. Not the other way around. So I'm the one who has the reasons to be angry. Not you."

Odd little puzzle pieces started falling into place for Katherine. "You're mad that I left?" she asked, amazement dripping from every word.

"Mad?" he responded. "*Mad* doesn't even cover half of it. We had an agreement. An *agreement.* But obviously your word means nothing to you."

The whole picture formed quickly. "Oh, I get it. We got so bogged down in everything that I forgot about our agreement. I forgot finding the best way to care for Jason was only half your agenda. I forgot you wanted to capitalize on this marriage for your new television station." She shook her head. "Now I understand why you're mad. Why you're brooding—sulking," she amended testily. "I've probably blown your chances to become the king of family-oriented television."

Another thought leapt to her brain. "And that's why you didn't go to the fund-raiser. If you're not going to create the new station, you don't need those legislators anymore," she surmised aloud. "Well, sorry, Alex, but both Jason and my sanity mean more to me than your making another couple million by fooling the public into thinking you're something that you really aren't."

For several seconds, he simply stared at her, his pain visible in his green eyes. The look on his face, the sadness in his eyes cut her to the quick so swiftly that she actually felt a keen embarrassment. Not only had she misread him, she'd insulted him. And he didn't deserve it. What she'd said was pure conjecture.

"After all the time we spent together you still see me as being that shallow?"

She swallowed. She hadn't seen him as being shallow in months. Loving. Thoughtful. Considerate. Yes. But shallow? Not at all. Suddenly she felt incredibly shallow herself.

She shook her head. "No."

Oddly enough, he seemed to believe her, but that didn't stop him from demanding an explanation. But he did it quietly, almost reverently, and in such a way that Katherine knew he would accept nothing less than the truth. "Then what did you think? And why did you leave?"

He turned away from her then, facing the window so that he could look out at the vast expanse of winter wonderland behind his home. The black tree trunks contrasted starkly with the pure white snow. The blue sky hung over the world like a protective blanket.

But Katherine didn't believe he'd turned away for the scenery. She'd hurt him. Not merely with what she'd just said, but also by leaving him. After years of living without a family, he'd created one for himself and with thoughts only for herself she'd destroyed it without an explanation, or even a conversation.

The very least she could do was tell him why.

Katherine took a deep breath. "It was the fact that I didn't find you shallow anymore that forced me to leave," she admitted softly.

"Really?" he asked skeptically, but still didn't turn to face her. "Somehow that's a little difficult to swallow."

"Alex," she said, her voice down to a frightened whisper. "Alex, this is so hard for me."

"I don't believe anything is hard for you," he said, finally turning to face her.

"Try living with you," Katherine said quietly.

He snorted a laugh. "I was the perfect gentleman."

"That's just it. You *were* the perfect gentleman. The perfect father. A wonderful cook. You were a shoulder to cry on. You were someone who listened. Someone who cared. For once in my life, I didn't feel like I was alone."

"And you found something bad in that?"

"No. I loved it," she admitted softly, then gathered her courage and decided that if she was making confessions she might as well get the whole mess out in the open. "I loved *you.*"

Her answer caused him to draw a sharp breath, and Katherine felt ready to die of embarrassment. If nothing else, that odd reaction was confirmation that the last thing he wanted to hear from her was a declaration of love, a woman who loved him would do nothing but tie him down.

"Look, forget I said that," she announced and rose from her seat. "I mean, we had a deal, and I blew it. I just wanted you to know that it wasn't you.... I mean, it wasn't what you think. You're wonderful, Alex. And I took you a little too seriously."

She turned and began to leave from the library, as much of her dignity intact as she could salvage. Across the room, in words so low and so full of emotion, they reached out to her like the caress of a longtime lover, he whispered, "I loved you, too, Katherine. Probably from the beginning. I fired poor Ralph for merely suggesting a prenuptial agreement."

Shocked, Katherine stopped her steps. She remembered hearing Ralph giving him the agreement and then never seeing the agreement, or Ralph again. Still, disbelief wouldn't allow her to turn around. Realism kept her in her place, literally and figuratively. Refusing to enter into a prenuptial agreement didn't necessarily mean he loved her. "Then why didn't you ever say it?"

Alex only stared at her for a minute. He could tell her he'd tried, but she'd always stopped him one second before he would have reached the obvious. Or he could tell her he wasn't sure about her feelings for him and didn't want to force them into an uncomfortable situation. Both of which were true. But both were also based on one simple fact. One painful fact.

He swallowed and decided he'd always been a gambling man. Now was not the time to lose his courage, not when everything he wanted was on the table.

"I always thought you wouldn't want to love me."

That turned her around. "I know some of the things Jessica told me caused me—"

He shook his head. "I was talking about the other things. The fact that I don't have a family...have absolutely no idea who my real father is."

"Oh, Alex, I don't care who your father is. I love you—the man you are now. To be honest, I don't even care about your reputation. Or even the things Jessica told me. I love you for who you are now, and who you'll be, not who you were."

It took him a few seconds to absorb all that, not because what she said was so difficult, but because it was so simple. It was simple and honest and came directly from her heart. More than that, it made him realize that for all his roaming and searching for adventure, this simplicity was all he'd really wanted.

"Come here," he said, nudging his head as an indicator that she should join him. "Gimme a kiss. A real kiss."

Katherine smiled, her heart seemed to take wings, her soul felt a release, a boundlessness like nothing she'd ever felt before. "My pleasure," she said, then moved into his arms to accept a kiss that expressed everything both had been too cautious to say and sometimes even too cautious to feel.

They were going to make it.

Katherine knew they were.

She would see to it.

*They would see to it,* she realized as he kissed her. They would make it in spite of his past, the complications of his money and all the pressures of his businesses, his life and raising Jason. Not to mention their own children...

She pulled away from him abruptly. "I think one of us had better go check on Jason and the other ought to go find Ronald."

"Now?" he asked incredulously.

"We're not going to manage kids, seventeen cars, two careers and six television stations without a little help."

He smiled, slowly, wonderfully. "No, I suppose we're not."

She kissed him then, her lips warm and soft, supple against his smooth mouth. "And we're also not going to get any privacy until Ronald gets here." She pressed her lips against his again, this time tracing a line from his ear to his collar bone with the long, red nail of her index finger. "You would like a little privacy, wouldn't you?"

Alex squeezed his eyes shut. "Thank God I bought Ronald that car phone for Christmas. He couldn't have gotten too far in twenty minutes."

"Good," Katherine purred, pulling out of his embrace. "After you apologize to Ronald and convince him to come back, relieve me in the family room with Jason, and I'll go upstairs and slip into something a little more comfortable."

Sliding her open palms down his chest, she moved away from him and walked to the door. Her hand on the doorknob she turned and smiled. "Like nothing."

He grabbed the receiver of the phone. "I'll hurry."

# *Epilogue*

When Judge Arnold Black entered his courtroom, he wasn't surprised to see Katherine and Alex. He was, however, slightly perplexed by the fact that they both seemed to have brought their own attorney. Except they were all scrambled up. Alex Cane was sitting by Attorney Munro. Katherine was beside Ralph Fasulo.

"Ladies and gentlemen," the judge greeted, striding to his desk, his robe billowing around him. After taking his seat, he added, "Counsel, present yourselves."

"Well, actually, we're both representing the Canes," Munro said, rising from his chair behind the Petitioner's table. The sound of his chair scraping against the tile floor echoed hollowly in the huge, empty courtroom.

Judge Black glanced at Ralph Fasulo, who hadn't risen and who didn't look nearly as sleek or slick as he had this time last August. In fact, he looked slightly humble. "Does Mr. Munro speak for you, Mr. Fasulo?"

"Yes, Your Honor," Ralph said, rising from his seat at the other end of the table.

"Good. Let's get down to business then." Sliding his glasses on his nose, Judge Black glanced down at his desk and picked up a group of legal documents. "The docket shows that Marissa Peligrini and her husband withdrew their petition for custody last March." He glanced at the foursome over the rim of his glasses. "You know anything about this, Mr. Cane?"

"Only that she and her husband were experiencing some financial difficulties, Your Honor."

"I see," he said, glancing down at the documents again. "I also have a petition filed in May that combines both of your requests for custody from last year into one petition, given that you are now married."

Munro rose. "Yes, Your Honor."

"Okay," the judge said, setting the new petition aside, then he looked up again. "And I take it all is happy on the marital front?"

"Fine, Your Honor," Munro said.

"I'd like Katherine to answer," the judge said, smiling craftily.

Looking chagrined, Katherine rose from her seat. Her protruding stomach balanced itself on the table. "Well, Your Honor, I'm not sure what you want me to say, but—"

"You're pregnant?" the judge asked.

"Due in October," Alex said, rising. "But that doesn't mean we won't be able to handle Jason. We have a manservant, Ronald, who is dedicated almost exclusively to assisting with the children."

"You're pregnant," Judge Black said again, misty-eyed with wonder that people could still surprise him after all these years. "Right from the beginning, I could have sworn you were trying to pull something over on me." He stopped, shook his head incredulously and faced them with a broad smile. "But you're really happily married."

"Couldn't be better, Your Honor," Alex said, grinning.

"Katherine?"

"Couldn't be better."

"Hearing's adjourned," the judge said, pounding his gavel. "I'll have my secretary type up the order granting custody and your attorney...*attorneys* will each get one in about a week."

"That's it?" Alex asked, stunned.

"Well, your next step is to file papers to adopt," the judge advised as he rose from his seat. "But for the time being you have indefinite, unprotested custody."

Alex bounded around the table and gave Katherine a huge hug. Then Munro hugged Katherine, as Ralph slapped Alex on the shoulder. Before they began walking back up the aisle to the double door entrance of the courtroom, the doors burst open and Jason shot through the opening, Ronald on his heels.

"Is it over, yet?" he asked eagerly.

"I'm sorry, sir," Ronald said, grabbing Jason's T-shirt and pulling him back to stand behind him. "I don't know why he's so energetic today."

"He's three, now, Ronald," Katherine said. "He's bigger and smarter and wants to do—"

"And I gave him a bowl of Cocoa Critters."

All eyes turned in Alex's direction.

"What?" Alex asked innocently. "We were watching cartoons. I wanted Cocoa Critters. I couldn't very well sit there and eat them in front of him."

"We could change *your* eating habits, sir."

"I don't want to change my eating habits."

Ronald smiled, hoisting Jason into his arms. "I know, but I'm the one who does the shopping."

* * * * *

# COMING NEXT MONTH

**#1114 DADDY ON BOARD—Terry Essig**

*Fabulous Fathers*

Lenore Pettit's son needed a father figure, and he picked her boss, Paul McDaniels. For Tim's sake she agreed to a vacation with Paul and his daughter. But they could never be a family—could they?

**#1115 THE COWBOY AND THE PRINCESS—Lindsay Longford**

Hank Tyler had nothing to offer a woman—he'd given up his heart long ago. And "princess" Gillian Elliott would certainly not be the exception. But Hank couldn't resist finding out if under the "princess" image lay a sweet and loving lady....

**#1116 ALONG COMES BABY—Anne Peters**

*First Comes Marriage*

When Ben Kertin found a pregnant woman hiding on his ranch he couldn't turn her away. Marcie Hillier needed protection, and marriage seemed the best solution. Until Ben began wishing for more than a temporary arrangement....

**#1117 WILD WEST WIFE—Jayne Addison**

Josh Spencer would never allow a woman to mess with his Wild West ranch! He was determined to show Carly Gerard, his new partner, that rodeos were not for city slickers. Until Josh began thinking of Carly in very wifely terms.

**#1118 FORTUNE'S BRIDE—Donna Clayton**

Dylan Mitchell had sworn off romance for life; he could take care of himself and his young daughter without anyone's help. Then Laura Adams inherited part of his company, and Dylan found himself falling for this bride of fortune!

**#1119 SECOND CHANCE FAMILY—Laura Anthony**

Single mom Savannah Markum needed help against cattle rustlers, but she hadn't counted on the inspector being her ex-fiancé, Matt Forrester. Savannah had vowed never to marry a lawman, but seeing Matt again made her wonder if their love deserved a second chance.